A. L. Barker left school when she was sixteen and, after the War, joined the BBC. Her debut collection of short stories, *Innocents*, won the first-ever Somerset Maugham Prize in 1947, her novel, *John Brown's Body*, was shortlisted for the Booker McConnell Prize in 1969 and *The Gooseboy* won the Macmillan Silver Pen Award in 1988.

A. L. Barker lives in Surrey.

"Page after brilliant page . . . what she does, she does better than anyone now writing."

Susan Hill

Being fiction as it is maybe
here and rather like biography,
and quite good
a lot here presented ?
+ i
changes!

A CASE EXAMINED

A. L. Barker

ARENA

An Arena Book
Published by Arrow Books Limited
62–65 Chandos Place, London WC2N 4NW

An imprint of Century Hutchinson Limited

London Melbourne Sydney Auckland
Johannesburg and agencies throughout
the world

First published by The Hogarth Press Ltd 1965
Arena edition 1989
© A. L. Barker 1965

Phototypeset by Input Typesetting Ltd, London
Printed and bound in Great Britain by
The Guernsey Press Co Ltd, Guernsey, C.I.

ISBN 0 09 956510 2

To the
ANONYMOUS DONOR
of the Cheltenham Award

Seventy per cent of writers never earn more than
£500 a year from their writing, and many always
earn less. They must work to live to write. If working
and living use a minimum of twelve hours a day,
that leaves them eight to sleep and four to write—
or four to sleep and eight to write—in theory, and
if no-one calls, no-one is ill, nothing burns or peters
out, it is not Christmas, nor holidays, they are not
tired and nothing stops them. They may try to write
on buses and in trains, standing, sitting, while the
dinner cooks, before the shopbell rings, in any and
every moment which can be got. It will depend on
the individual conscience whether the moment is
redeemed or filched. Time to write in peace is what
seventy per cent of writers want and do not get.

I should like to think that this book is the better
for being the product of time neither redeemed nor
filched, but generously bestowed.

Contents

PART ONE

Rose Antrobus said, "Why do you like that view?" and Eric Cade turned with his gauche, guilty start. "Whenever you come here you go and look out of that window. It's not the best view, either."

"It's the best view from where I'm standing—from the Ebone Street end."

She went to the window and looked with him.

"The potting-shed, my clothes-post, redcurrants rampant—it's only another version of somewhere back of—where was it?"

"Ebone Street, my first parish."

She nodded. "If you want contrast, why not the morning-room window? You can look across the lawn to the Weald, we had the house built so that you could. It's one of the amenities and we'd list it if we were selling."

"But you don't see what I see." He was tiresome when he would not take a teasing. Rose sometimes thought that to struggle so much was a sign of weakness. "Of course we none of us see alike, even shapes get interpreted. The shed, the clothes-post, the currant bushes—there, I suppose, you'd stop. But I go on, I see the path, how neat the path is, unbroken, and how clean. The rain has washed off even the surface dust. You could eat your dinner off that path—" he smiled wanly—"I'd do better, anyway, to trust it than some of the plates at some of the places—And the flower-beds are forked over, I don't see weeds, only plants thriving as the seed packets said they would. I see the shed which you use only for putting earth into pots and plants into the earth and I see it's well built and newly painted. The fruit bushes are budding, there'll be redcurrant jelly and blackcurrant pie when the time comes. It's the ideal outlook, what we'd all like to see at our backs. We'd know we were all right everywhere then." He said stiffly, "Pardoning the word, it's a sublime view."

"I like things to be nice. So does Ted. Do we have to answer for that?"

"Of course not." He began walking up and down, striking his heels urgently into the pile of the carpet. "We'd all like things to be nice and I think that's our salvation."

"Then why aren't we saved? All of us? Will you have more coffee?"

"Please." He stopped at the other end of the room and looked at her with guilt poking out all over him. "It really is good of you to give me lunch."

"Nonsense, it's the obvious thing to do. There's no time between the end of your Council meeting and the start of the Self-Help Committee for you to get lunch, whereas I have no one but myself to cater for at midday and I'm glad of an incentive. We'll consider it a standing arrangement before each Committee meeting."

"Rose, I wasn't criticising you; oh, Heaven knows—"

"If you had been, I would have answered your criticism."

It was a habit of his not to let well alone. "We aren't all saved because we don't know how to make things nice or we haven't the will to. But we do want to. Witness the Peacheys."

"You're going to have to make up your mind about them."

He took refuge in drinking his coffee, and Rose sighed. "I must go and set out the chairs."

"I'll help you." He drained his cup and, putting it down, was bothered by the uncleared lunch-table. "What about all this?"

"Mrs Gibb will see to it."

He knew there was Mrs Gibb, he had seen her minutes ago, did he suppose there was time, anyway, to do the washing-up before these women arrived? It was not insincerity in him, but a being slightly out of touch. He often let himself in for unnecessary trouble from people who could not or would not bridge the gap for him.

"You'll have to help me with the meeting," she said, putting her arm in his and turning him, because he was still hovering, towards the morning-room. "I think it's going to be difficult. I'm not sure now that it was a good idea to have it here."

"Why not?" He said, as he opened the door, "This is such a pleasant room, even committee work will be a pleasure in it." He was struck by another thought which arrested him on the threshold. "Are you thinking of wear and tear? Possible damage? Rose, I'm sure we'll all be very careful, oh indeed—But of course there might be marks just from the passage of six—or is it seven?—pairs of shoes across the carpet—"

"I'm not concerned about any such thing. How ridiculous." Rose drew the chairs into a semicircle. "It seemed only sensible at the time, there being so few of us. I can't see the Committee getting under way, can you, in a corner of the church hall, with no heating?"

"It really is uneconomical to start the boiler just for one hour's warmth. If we could have met on a Thursday, before the Fellowship Tea—"

"We couldn't. Only without Mrs Betts, and I do think she's important." Rose, having plumped cushions, went to the mirror and lifted her chin at her reflection. "It's a question of diplomacy. The last thing I want is to seem as if I'm trying to keep the Fund under my thumb, but as Hilda's executor my duty is to see that it's properly administered."

"You would hardly have formed a committee if you wanted complete control."

"Will that cut as much ice with the committee meeting under my own roof? You know how susceptible some of these women are." She smiled wryly into the mirror. "I must try to be discreet and not put my oar in too often. It will be up to you, Eric, to draw them off a little."

"My own attitude, or what my attitude ought to be, isn't clear to me yet."

"I intend to be practical," Rose said mildly, "but it's no use asking you to be."

The ladies all arrived within the next few minutes. There were six of them, not young, not yet beginning to be seriously old, of an age and disposition for it not to show greatly or matter much whether it was forty or fifty they were pushing. They were Rose's contemporaries and really, she thought, theirs was an excellent time of life. She could say for herself that she would never have it better, not too much, as youth had been, and not too little, as old age would be.

She wondered if they thought so too and looked, as she greeted them, for satisfaction in their faces. She could not see it, although Miss Havelock had a complacency imposed on her by her fat: there was no room, with so much flesh to accommodate, for any disruption. The others looked as if they were still on the track of something in a general way, except for little Mavis Tyndall, whose face was laced-up for something particular.

They subsided into Rose's chairs like a flock of birds into a field of corn. They wore their best hats and pearls and too much powder. Mrs Choules, the butcher's wife, was a dusky mauve under hers.

"Vicar," she said to Cade, "my husband wants me to take you to task about those flats next to us."

"Me, Mrs Choules?"

"I'm told they're church property."

"If they are, they belong to the Church Commissioners and not to St John's."

"Haven't you got any pull with the Commissioners?"

"My dear Mrs Choules, I haven't even got a string."

"I don't think it is church property," said Rose. "Ted says the block is owned by a syndicate. What's the trouble, anyway?"

"They're letting in the blacks. One of those men that wraps his head like a pudding has taken a flat there."

"That will be Dr Ahmed," said Cade. "He's a chiropodist."

"But Vicar, I call a spade a spade," said Mrs Choules, frisking the violets on her bosom, "and I call that the thin end of the tarbrush."

And charity, a kind of loving, is what we're here for, thought Rose. The idea amused her, she smiled in Mrs Choules' face.

Mrs Choules looked back blankly for a moment, then she gave one of her chesty laughs. "That's me, I have to speak

14

out. My husband says I won't make friends that way but I'll find out who my enemies are."

There was an undue pause until Mrs Betts, enlarging her drawl, said, "Rose, how come we haven't seen Ted at the Club?"

"He's been working the last two week-ends, Sue."

"He should work at his golf, he's not the world's best player."

Rose saw that Mrs Choules was gazing about as if she were pricing the furniture and Mavis Tyndall was giving alarmed bobbing looks at everything from under her hat. Victorine Gregory put up her hand like a schoolgirl.

"May I smoke?"

"You know you can, Vee. The idea is to be comfortable. After all, it's going to be a small chore administering this Fund and I don't see why you should be troubled in the flesh as well as in the spirit."

"I need hardly tell you it's a matter of economy," said Cade, sitting down in their midst with a great rustle of practicality. "Tuesday is a blank day for the church hall, no one uses it and we should need a day's fuel to get heat up for our one hour in the afternoon. As things stand—as they've always stood, I believe, even before my time?' He waited, brows raised, placing the ball far back in their court, but the ladies sat stolidly, with bunched or spreading thighs, and let it lie. "Not a new state of affairs, at any rate, nothing individual," he looked from face to face with a confederate air, "and we must bear with it, I must ask you to bear—"

"If Mrs Antrobus hadn't suggested it, I should have," said Mrs Choules. "I'd have had you all round to our place because I couldn't sit five minutes in that cold barracks of a church hall, not with my chest."

"Why not cover the cost of the heating out of the Fund?" said Miss Havelock.

Rose nodded, to herself more than Miss Havelock whom she had invited on the Committee because she was reputed to be a sound business woman. "I suppose that would be admissible."

"Not that I've any objection to meeting here."

"It's nice of Rose to have us," said Victorine Gregory. Ash fell from her cigarette and she ground it into the carpet with her shoe. "Conscientious, too, because there's nothing to stop her doling out the money wherever she chooses. Or not doling it."

Eric Cade flung up his head. "What do you mean, Mrs Gregory?"

"If it was me, I'd take something for my trouble. A pair of gloves, a new bag, tickets for the theatre—I'd dip in now and then. Rose won't." Victorine sucked at her cigarette: the compulsive rubbing and dusting of her fingers was getting more noticeable, was, in fact, impossible to ignore. "Rose won't touch a penny of it. She's incorruptible and don't any of you think, 'Well, she can afford to be'."

"I don't like the thoughts you're putting into my head, Vee," said Sue Betts. "They're on the bitchy side."

"I don't know where this is leading us," Cade was looking round as if for a signpost. "But it's nowhere I want to go."

"Vee's teasing us," said Rose. "We'll have to get used to it."

Victorine looked at her with eyes wincing against her own cigarette-smoke. "Rose turns the other cheek and shuts me up."

Rose said, "Perhaps we ought to talk about the Fund seriously now. You've all been good enough to come here for that purpose. I've christened us the Self-Help Committee and we shall be an *ad hoc* committee, lasting as long as the Fund does. But there's no need to be rigidly official, is there? It would be nice if we kept our meetings a little more social than the Guild or the W.I. reckon to be, don't you think?"

"Social?" Miss Havelock made the word bristle.

"A relaxed atmosphere is what I'd like. It should be the most productive and it would, so to speak, be in context." Rose smiled. "Hilda was herself a thoroughly relaxed person. You all know about her Fund. She left the interest on certain of her investments until such time as her heir comes of age, when the interest will revert to him, to be used for the benefit of our church of St John's-on-the-Green

16

and its parishioners. As her executor it's my duty and intention to see that the money is used as she wished. But that's something I couldn't do alone. I'd never be sure I'd located all the deserving cases, far less examined and evaluated them fairly."

Miss Havelock's sigh gusted out of her huge body. "When does the legatee come of age?"

"Hilda's nephew is fourteen. We have seven years to benefit."

"By how much?"

"I thought of coming to that as Committee business, to keep some sort of sequence for the records. We must have records," said Rose.

Miss Havelock expended the last of her sigh with a faint whistle which was curiously flattening. "The lesser the sum the more difficult to administer. This sort of thing can be very tedious."

Rose felt chastened. The new minute book which she held on her knee, ruled and headed, "Self-Help Committee meeting (first), Tuesday, April 4th", looked naïve. The ladies, brought out in their best hats too soon after lunch she felt would consider it an imposition, the goodness of their hearts being bespoke. She said, smiling round at them, "It won't be as much fun as a bridge party."

Victorine said, "Virtue being its own reward."

"We're here to help, honey," said Sue Betts. "You go right ahead and lay it on the table."

"Is it agreed then," said Rose, "that the first thing we should do is elect a chairman?"

"Ratify, not elect," Cade called out. "The choice is surely made?"

Miss Havelock frowned. "Committee work may be tiresome, but unless it is done in open session it loses justification."

"I think Vicar should be chairman," said Mrs Choules.

"No!" Cade held up one angular hand, palm out, with a policing rather than a pious gesture. "That would be completely unethical."

"Oh why, Eric?" Rose put down her notebook as if she

17

did not expect to be soon convinced. "I think it's an excellent proposal."

"As a potential beneficiary perhaps I shouldn't even be on the Committee?"

"You, Vicar? A beneficiary? Well, you're certainly deserving—"

"I represent St John's, I'm answerable for the fabric of the church as well as the souls of its parishioners." He turned to Rose. "Under the terms of the Fund it's not inconceivable that St John's itself may at some time benefit?"

Rose said gravely, "It's certainly not inconceivable. Hilda did in fact put it in that sequence—'. . . the benefit of our church of St John and its parishioners'."

"You be chairman, Rose," said Sue Betts. "Look what friends you and Hilda were."

"Oh, Hilda would have wished it." Victorine Gregory butted one cigarette into the lighted end of another.

"We should put it to the vote—"

"Rose for chairman: all in favour say aye—" Victorine held up the scarlet cigarette-stub.

Sue Betts said "Aye, aye", and after a moment Mrs Choules patted her bosom and said, "Oh, pardon me—aye," on the crest of her indigestion.

Miss Havelock, looking at Rose accommodated a faint gleam on her face. That, and a grunt signified her acquiescence. Mavis Tyndall pressed her lips tight and nodded violently.

"It goes without saying that I'm for Mrs Antrobus—a vote of confidence indeed. And *ex-officio*, of course, as Mrs Loeb's executor, I think she ought to take the chair." Cade rubbed his palms thankfully over his knees. "Rose, the Committee is now yours."

"It always was," murmured Victorine.

"Do be quiet, Vee,' said Rose. "I think we should be serious."

They were looking at her and she was aware, as always when she faced a number of women, of the barrage. It was a united effort, Mavis Tyndall and the Havelock woman putting up their fire together. Once Rose would have been

18

intimidated. She would have worried and let it dwindle her and tried to hit on some catalyst, a word or formula dear to them all which would transmute their antagonism *en masse* into warm humanity, or just a favourable disposition. But she had realised early in her committee life that the barrage was an instinctive thing, and impersonal. It got up, quite naturally, like hackles, at sight of another woman, any woman, on a platform—actual or implied—to tell them what to think or do. She noted the same reaction in herself. The defence, failing oratory which she did not have, was to isolate and crumble. There were always opponents, a hard core or a lifeless lump. They sorted themselves out and they would do that, thought Rose, even from this small chosen group.

"Thank you for your vote of confidence. I shall try to justify it." She tapped her minute book. "I propose, if you all agree, to take notes of our meetings. Mrs Loeb's executors will want to see them."

"The minutes should be circulated to the Committee first," said Miss Havelock. "We may wish to make amendments."

"Of course. I'll send copies to you all." Rose smiled at Mrs Choules, who did her husband's accounts on a comptometer. "I'm not good with machines, but if I can coax four carbons out of my typewriter it will mean typing the minutes twice only. Now the sum available—" Rose addressed herself pleasantly to Miss Havelock—"amounts this quarter to forty-eight pounds, four shillings and four pence. Next quarter we may have a little less or a little more, subject to market fluctuations. But I think we can expect the interest to remain constant in the region of fifty pounds a quarter."

"It's not going to send anyone over the rainbow, is it?" said Sue Betts.

"We haven't all got eighty-carat rainbows, honey," said Victorine.

"*I* shouldn't let it go begging," said Mrs Choules.

"Nor me." Victorine grimaced round her cigarette. "It would be something not to go cap in hand for."

"I think it's a serviceable little sum. It won't change anybody's life," said Rose, "but it could ease a burden, relieve a worry or simply help someone to keep going."

"Candidates?" asked Miss Havelock.

"There are two. First, the Peacheys."

"The what?"

"A family by the name of Peachey."

Sue Betts said, "Back home we say a thing's peachy if it's pretty nice."

"They aren't pretty or nice, poor things." In her notebook Rose had written: "Chairman—R. Antrobus elected". Under this she wrote: "Decisions—(1) The Peacheys". "It's quite a sad case. There's the mother, still just a girl, and three young children, aged six, four and a baby of six months." Rose lifted her shoulders and sighed round at them all. "The husband was committed to a criminal lunatic asylum four months ago for assaulting an elderly woman."

"Sex crime?"

"I don't think so, Vee. He didn't know her, he'd never seen her before. It happened in Wolverhampton or somewhere north—"

"Accrington," murmured Cade.

"The point being that there was no reason for what he did. He had a brainstorm, a sort of *crise de tête*."

"She was laughing at him," said Mavis Tyndall.

They raised their eyebrows, quite startled. Miss Havelock put three chins down into her neck and turned her humid moon of a face. After one wild upward glance Mavis Tyndall stared fixedly at the floor. Rose could not remember at that moment why she had invited her to join the Committee. There was no room for anyone who carried such little weight, who was quite pathologically small. Then she remembered Eric Cade's proposing her. What was it he had said? "Mrs Tyndall has energy and conscience and doesn't pride herself on anything. She could be useful to you."

She had been already, or so Rose hoped. But that aggressive humility of hers would be wearying in committee, Rose didn't want to have to be continually raising her up.

"Mrs Tyndall's been to see the Peacheys and the eldest

20

child is in her Sunday-school class. She knows more about them than I do."

She really had little to pride herself on. Her face drew to a point, nose, mouth and chin, like a mouse's and probably, thought Rose, she had the kind of energy for pedalling round and round on a wheel.

"Would you tell us what you know, Mavis?"

The "Mavis", perhaps, started her on the wrong foot, because she addressed herself to Rose and desperately ignored the faces left and right of her.

"They both come to Sunday school now, both the children, the little girl as well as the boy. She's only four, but she's very good, she sits so still. I don't think a child ought to sit like that for an hour at a time, she doesn't get up to sing with the others or look at the Bible pictures. The only time she moves is when she comes in and when she goes out, it isn't natural in a child that age—"

"She keeps pretty clean though, doesn't she?"

"Clean?" Mavis Tyndall went on staring, reddening and staring at Rose as if it were she who had spoken.

Rose smiled gently. "Mrs Gregory's children never stay still for a minute."

Victorine leaned into Mrs Tyndall's range. "Don't you ever wish yours would cut down on the laundry?"

Some of the fire died out of Mavis Tyndall's face. "I have no children."

"Well now," said Rose pacifically, "could we hear a report on your visit to Mrs Peachey? I don't think anyone else, except Mr Cade, knows the family. We need to be put in the picture, that's why I suggested you go and see them."

"I'd have gone anyway, about the child. I'm worried about the child—" She could see that they weren't. Why should they be? They hadn't seen what she had seen and she couldn't tell them. What words could she use? She sought, painfully and openly, for words of some acceptable sort and they came out stilted and impersonal because it was a "report" Rose had asked for and these ladies did not sit in Sunday school.

"I visited Mrs Peachey on the 25th of March. She was

21

unco-operative at first, she said she had nothing to add to the statement she had made about her husband. I assured her I did not represent the police nor the National Assistance Board nor any welfare organisation already known to her. She then explained that she was tired and upset because the baby had been ill all night and the milkman would not carry up the morning milk—"

"What?"

"She lives in a Council flat on the fifth floor. She claims that her neighbours are prejudiced on account of her husband and that they influence the delivery men against her."

"Do you think that's true?"

Mavis Tyndall laced her fingers in her lap. "As I left, the woman from the flat below came out and said, 'Why don't you fuss after decent people for a change? That lot up there should be smoked out'."

Decent people did not need looking after. There was something indecent about being in want, a universal prejudice. Rose could trace it back in her own mind to something from the Bible about being 'hungry and ye fed me, naked, and ye clothed me'. In the nakedness, the cold dirty skinniness, was the indecency.

"What sort of a woman is Mrs Peachey?"

"Not more than twenty-two or three. And hard—young people are."

That, Rose could appreciate, would have been Mrs Tyndall's experience, and in the fifth-floor Council flat with the baby grizzling and the indecent wants she had taken knocks which she was prepared to excuse or glorify by putting them down to youth.

"She told me her husband had been studying to take a degree—by post."

Coming from hard, young Mrs Peachey it would have been a statement of fact, respect or pity to be supplied by the hearer. From Mavis Tyndall it had a futile, catchpenny sound.

"He wanted to better himself, he wanted to better all of them, she said, and he was overworking. He felt dizzy and sometimes he fainted in the street. There was some persecution, people pointing and talking about him—"

"They talk about me," said Mrs Choules. "I don't call it persecution."

"Mrs Peachey said they're disliked by a lot of people but her husband believed they were hated by everyone."

"Why should they be disliked? Before anything had happened, I mean?" Rose was doodling, drawing bad circles in her notebook. "One can understand people turning against them afterwards, after what he did to that woman. But at first, when they were all together, don't you think that then it was just a complex? An excuse for not doing as well as they might have? There's no reason, leaving aside the other business, why they should be unpopular. Is there? Mavis?"

She must have been thinking unhappily along her own lines, well along, because she was brought back with a jerk, her long mouse's nose twitching hopelessly. "I don't think so—I don't know—"

"Eric? Do you know of any reason?"

Rose asked him as a matter of form, politeness before the others, because if he knew any reason he was in honour bound not to give it. An awkward situation—perhaps he really shouldn't be on the Committee.

Cade said, "I think their trouble has been that they've tried too hard—"

"Oh, sure!" cried Sue Betts. 'Peachey tried hard when he beat that poor woman nearly to death. If anyone ought to be helped, she did."

"Peachey's wife and children are innocent of his crime," said Cade, "but they may have to suffer for it more than he will."

"Are they starving?" said Miss Havelock briskly.

"Of course not. Mrs Peachey gets National Assistance."

"Then what will forty-eight pounds do for them?"

"In a household like that, money is always useful."

Rose said, "Mrs Tyndall has definite ideas. May we hear them, Mavis?"

"They have no proper furniture, there was never enough money to buy it with the children coming so quickly—"

23

"They had to get married in a hurry, of course?"

Mrs Choules, Rose noticed, had a wolfish smile for one with such a bulbous face.

Looking round at them all, Mavis Tyndall seemed to see that she needed to take up arms. She laid her words down with their edges out.

"They have one large bed, two chairs and a table. The rest is boxes and crates. The baby sleeps in a box and the two other children in the bed with their mother. When Denis Peachey was at home they were put at the bottom between their parents' feet. They have no decent crockery, everything is cracked and chipped. Mrs Peachey has one bowl for washing up and bathing the baby—"

"When Hartley and I got married," said Sue Betts, "we couldn't afford even the dime-store stuff. We used to get factory throw-outs, and we had a lot of fun matching up."

"The children haven't enough clothes, they wear the same coats winter and summer. They have no toys, the boy runs in the street and the little girl sits at home just as she does in Sunday school. She has no will, no wish, even. We can only try what we know," said Mrs Tyndall, as if she had come to the bitter heart of her matter. "When something, someone, won't go, we can only wind it up and hope the wheels will start turning. I bought her a doll. She was frightened of it, her mother said she thought it was dead."

Mavis Tyndall had not been a good person to send. She was woolly about the child, one child, and nothing else counted with her. That was a luxury which the Committee could not afford to indulge her in. Charity should be objective, should be deserved—that was to say, there should be some foreseeable return in moral fibre or regeneration. One would like, certainly Rose would like in the matter of Hilda Loeb's bequest, to prove benefit, afterwards to produce on the one hand so much money, on the other so much good.

"You can see this money being used by Mrs Peachey," Rose said, "and not just spent?"

"I can't be sure, of course, but I hope—"

She was honest: as far as she went she could be relied

24

upon to do her best. The question to be decided was how much her best was worth, this time and any other.

"I hope she'll buy things that National Assistance won't pay for. She's at the end of her tether, she's lost her husband, he may never come back. She doesn't know why she's trying now, or what for, and I'm afraid she'll stop soon," said Mrs Tyndall, herself stopping, with her eyes on Rose's face.

"And you believe that forty-eight pounds might restore her purpose in life?"

Rose spoke without irony, but she realised that it was an indication to the meeting that there was already a prevailing wind and which way it blew: no harm in that at this stage. Mrs Tyndall was not a powerful speaker, but she had the human case to plead, a strong one that could get half-way home on statement alone.

"No, only her husband could do that." Mavis Tyndall looked steadily, with rising colour, at all the ladies. "She's young, she wants him badly, she wants no one else—"

"Not the children?" said Victorine.

"She'd let them go, I think she'd let everything go if she stopped trying. I'm afraid for the children." She had been pushing it from the start, but this was her strongest thrust yet. " 'In care', they call it, don't they, when they have to take children from their mothers and put them in homes?"

"What sort of things," said Miss Havelock, "won't National Assistance pay for?"

"Things we take for granted. You and I use cups that are whole and plates that aren't cracked, we have a nice set of saucepans to cook with—"

Rose smiled. Mavis Tyndall making common ground with Miss Havelock over saucepans struck her as absurd.

"Ordinary things, 'necessities' we call them, tools for the job, and we don't think what it would be like doing the job without them. Even a coat—" She touched her own lapels. "A decent coat is a necessity. The money couldn't give her a reason to live but it would give her heart."

There was a pause and Rose left it with them. To disengage from Mavis Tyndall's gaze she got up and went to the window. There had been rain before lunch, enough to rinse

25

the air. Under the white spring sky her garden was folded and mitred and the earth drawn tidy. A 'sublime' view? How much was one entitled or common-sensibly required to take for granted?

She looked round at the ladies. "I should perhaps remind you that once the money is paid to the beneficiary we have no further say in how it is spent. We can't make conditions, let alone try to get them kept. It will be up to Mrs Peachey to do with it as we think best."

"I believe she will," said Mrs Tyndall. "She'll want to."

"We must hope so," Rose said, "for the sake of the children."

Cade joined her at the window. Seeing him fingering his empty pipe, she asked, "Would it upset any of us if Mr Cade smoked?"

He seemed not to hear. He went on rubbing his thumb round the bowl of the pipe and the words, 'Virgin briar' passed through Rose's mind and amused her in passing. Thorny he was in his way, with the barbs turned inwards so that nothing went smoothly for him. Celibacy she had settled on him long ago.

He said over his shoulder, "I think it just the kind of marginal case that Mrs Loeb meant to provide for."

Miss Havelock looked at her watch. "And the other claimant?"

" 'Candidate' is the better word," said Rose, "and I'm putting it forward myself since I couldn't get Mr Cade to. It's our own church, St John's-on-the-Green. I'll ask Mr Cade to state the case even though he feels he can't plead it."

Rose could not make up her mind whether Cade, turning from the window was shamming reluctance. She hoped so because no man in his position had any right to be self-effacing. It was going to be tedious if she had to contend with him for his own benefit.

"It won't engage your interest so much—I trust it won't engage your self-interest." He reddened, he was going to put the case badly because it embarrassed him. "We need new hassocks for the pews—" It embarrassed him because he had some notion that it was ridiculous for their knees to be comfortable and sublime for Mrs Peachey to be comforted. 'Sublime'—he had already broken in the word this afternoon. "It is a rather—frivolous need."

Rose said, "I don't agree. I think it's essential. The things we kneel on are disintegrating and dirty and there are only enough to furnish three pews."

"Hassocks?" said Victorine.

Cade put in quickly, "They're the least of our worries. I'm much more concerned about the boilers—"

"Some of the older members of the congregation actually find it painful to say their prayers."

Victorine laughed. It was possible, Rose thought, to dislike one's friends.

"The fact that we may all be poisoned by coke fumes next winter shouldn't influence us. Of course there would be no problem if we had five hundred pounds to bestow instead of fifty."

"If I took Mrs Loeb's forty-eight pounds, four shillings and four-pence," said Cade, "it would be a drop in the ocean."

"That's a little ungracious, don't you think, Eric?" said Rose, smiling.

"I didn't mean—"

"We'll discuss the pros and cons of course." Rose went to the door and called, "Mrs Gibb, I think we could do with some tea."

Mrs Choules swivelled round to Sue Betts. "I can promise those Easter lilies I spoke about. A customer of ours is getting them over from Guernsey."

"That's lovely," said Sue. "They're much more spiritual than daffs and there's nothing like being topical—if anyone notices."

"I shall," said Victorine. "Lilies make me feel fleshly."

"Could you be fleshly, honey?"

"It takes a flower to show me up, anyway."

Mavis Tyndall was listening as to a clash of giants, but Miss Havelock tapped with her finger-nail on a brass ashtray and made it ring like a bell.

"Is anyone going to plead the church's cause?"

"We're all personally acquainted with it," said Rose.

"I've stopped getting on my knees," said Mrs Choules. "I know some people feel they must, but you can be reverent if you can get your head down."

"I squat," said Victorine, "like a monkey."

"Could the money be found any other way?"

"Eventually. It would mean more jumbles and sales of work."

"We are called the 'Self-Help' Committee," said Victorine.

"It's quite shameful that in a parish such as ours any of the church furnishings should be so squalid—"

"Speaking as the church mouse," said Victorine, "we shouldn't have to go to the parish while there's such a strong smell of money in the congregation."

"Hilda would have given it. She always said she wouldn't get to Heaven if she didn't buy in. She was fixing to do something about those kneeling-pads—"

"The dead don't vote—at least, they shouldn't."

Rose was getting vexed with Victorine Gregory. She reminded herself that Victorine was going through a bad phase. A germ of something was infecting her being: she liked stroking people the wrong way, and lately it had become an ungentle rubbing. She wasn't so amusing about it either now, her nerves were frayed—and charred, thought Rose, seeing her crush out another cigarette. She was slightly over the edge, ready to be riled as well as to rile.

Rose had seen to it that tea should be aesthetically as well as physically stimulating. The china was her nice Coalport, the shallow cups so fine that a finger showed through like a bruise. Everything else was Victorian silver, teapot, cream-jug, spoons and cake-baskets. Rose had a weakness for Victoriana at its most flowery.

A rustle went over the ladies at sight of the tea-trolley. They adjusted their hats and shook out the lapels of their jackets. There was a sturdy wave of perfume and then Cade lit his pipe and the room smelt right, Rose thought, for business.

28

"Quite a party," said Victorine, coming to the trolley.

"Do help, not hinder me, Vee," murmured Rose.

Victorine put down a cup and saucer which she could not keep from chattering in her hand. "Since you ask," she said clearly, "mine is a floating vote at the moment."

Rose felt her temper ebb sharply. They were all looking, Cade took his pipe out of his mouth and rounded his lips like a fish. She could not keep the colour from rising to her face, knowing that she looked put out was enough to put her out.

She picked up the cup and saucer Victorine had laid down and looked into Miss Havelock's slit stare.

"Milk or lemon? Mrs Gibb is bringing China tea for anyone who prefers it."

After that the mood of the meeting sharpened and not even tea could relax it. There seemed to be an impression—which of course Victorine Gregory had given—that sides had been taken and that the situation was loaded. They sensed politics, and if to Mrs Choules it looked important to get into the right party, to a timid sort like Mavis Tyndall it would seem quite reckless to be in the wrong one.

Miss Havelock called out, "Mrs Antrobus, I have another appointment at 3.45. Do you think we could settle this matter before I go?"

"Of course. We'll put it to the vote now."

"Secret ballot?" said Victorine.

"Do you think that's necessary?"

Victorine smiled. "There may be some people here who are afraid of you, Rose."

"Afraid of me? How ridiculous!" Rose looked round for their laughter. Only Cade grinned feebly, and Rose couldn't help it, she cried, "That makes me feel utterly miserable!"

"Why, honey?" said Sue Betts kindly. "Don't you like to think you're a power?"

"Very well, we'll each take a slip of paper and write on it, 'Mrs Peachey', or 'Church'."

Rose went to her writing-table. She really was put out now, she knew whom she had to thank for it, but she blamed herself for asking Victorine Gregory on to the Committee.

She had thought she was doing a kindness. An aim, however small, it had seemed to her, might still some of that self-disruption, but now she could see that Victorine's trouble was the kind that reaches out and makes more.

"I shan't exercise my vote," said Cade. Rose turned to look at him. "It wouldn't be—just."

"You have a duty to your flock," said Victorine, "the kneelers. Surely you'd vote for them?"

"I have duties," said Cade, "and am divided between them."

"It will cost us our deciding vote," said Rose, tearing paper into strips, "but of course you must do as you think right. Now we'll write down our decisions and put the strips into this rose bowl. I take it we've all reached a decision, or been frightened into one?"

"We'll disguise our handwriting."

"This isn't a game, Vee." Rose gave each of them a slip of paper and a pencil. "Does anyone feel the need of more facts before deciding?"

Sue Betts was already scribbling. "Honey, this isn't the Rockefeller Trust."

Rose thought, they're impatient now, someone looks at her watch and they think of the time though they all have more than they know what to do with. They can't wait to make up their minds, they'll jump to conclusions.

"We might bear in mind," she said, looking round at them, "that since the sum of money involved is not great we should be the more careful to bestow it sensibly. As Miss Havelock says, the lesser the sum the more difficult it is to administer."

"No problem so far as I'm concerned." Sue Betts dropped her paper into the rose bowl. "And if anyone wants to know how I figure it I'll be glad to say."

Mrs Choules drained her tea-cup. " 'Hassocks', was it, we were to put?"

Victorine said to Rose, " 'Though I have all faith, so that I could remove mountains, and have not charity, I am nothing.' "

Rose wrote on her own paper, folded it and put it in the

30

bowl. She went over to Cade, who was looking out of the window.

"Will you count the votes?"

"Do you think I should?"

She said, sharply, so that they all glanced up, "Would you be tempted to swing the count?"

Cade's nose lifted with surprise. 'Yes—the other way."

"That's hypocrisy." She was vexed when he nodded. "Well, what do you want me to think? You're not a cynic— I hope you're not working up to anything, Eric, there's no virtue in being misunderstood."

She led him back to the table to count the votes. They were even: three for the church and three for Mrs Peachey.

"What now?" said Victorine. "Do we split the money or start a jackpot?"

Rose did not say she had been afraid of this. It would be like saying, 'I told you so', and they had every right to differ—in equal or unequal ratios.

"We must have a majority."

"How can we?"

"Vicar must vote," said Mrs Choules. "After all, he is on the Committee."

Cade moved his hands as if he were parting waters. "That I cannot do."

"Principles are the devil, aren't they?" said Victorine to Rose.

"I agree it would be easier if more of us had none."

"Maybe someone will change her mind," said Sue Betts.

Miss Havelock stirred. Through her enormous body a tremor went, she was preparing to stand up, to depart. Rose resented the air of physical disassociation this gave to the proceedings, of brushing off something as irrelevant now as the biscuit crumbs in her lap.

"I see no reason to change my mind. The money should go to the woman."

Rose was surprised. "You think so?"

"Why do you say it like that?"

"I wouldn't have thought—Oh, it doesn't matter. Of course one can't change one's mind at this stage—"

"I put people first, Mrs Antrobus," said Miss Havelock sternly. "Especially when there is a time factor—people are at a particular disadvantage there. In this case, as I understand it, time is limited, may indeed be almost run out on the one hand, and on the other is fairly indefinite. In other words," said Miss Havelock, simplifying, "this woman should be helped now or it may be too late, whereas the hassocks have been worn out for years and we are only just complaining."

"If that were so," said Rose, "we might compliment ourselves on our patience. Mr Cade knows as well as I do that we haven't suffered in silence. We can continue to penalise the old and infirm who find it difficult even to walk to church by making them kneel down on the stones when they get there, but should we say we're doing so because they have more time?"

"Where the emotions are concerned time is not calculable," said Miss Havelock.

"How true?" cried Rose. "And I should so like her to have the money! What are a few hassocks compared with the chance of giving someone the will to—" She did not say 'live', that was overdoing it—"the will to go on? But isn't there a danger that it might do the reverse and make her thoroughly dissatisfied? People like that don't always know how to receive—"

"We're talking about one woman, Rose, about Mrs Peachey. Remember?"

"And Mrs Peachey, being human, and with a sympathetic ear to unburden herself to, might become hysterical and say things she didn't mean. It's natural, isn't it, under a strain like this must be?"

"And the chance of fifty pounds if she laid it on thick enough," put in Mrs Choules bluntly.

"I'm saying," said Rose, "that she would, understandably, have made the most of her troubles to Mrs Tyndall. Wouldn't we all, in her circumstances?"

"She wasn't hysterical, she's not the type!"

Mavis Tyndall perhaps was. She had gone scarlet and

altogether too brilliant in the face for one so mousey. "And I didn't at any time mention the money."

"How do we know she won't blow it on clothes and men?" demanded Sue Betts. "If she's young and deprived, like you say, that's what she'll do."

"Men? There are no men—she loves her husband, she wants him back. She's young, yes, she'll hope if she's allowed to. And why shouldn't she buy clothes? She needs clothes, she's only got one old raincoat to her back. A raincoat!" cried Mrs Tyndall. "All through the winter!"

"What about the children?" asked Mrs Choules.

"She wouldn't spend it all on herself—I'm sure she wouldn't. But don't you see, it would give her a lift to have a few of the things she wants for herself? It would hearten her when she needs it most. If she loses heart, if she gives up—" Mrs Tyndall looked from face to face. "It's the children I'm thinking of."

"What are you thinking of, Rose?" said Victorine.

Rose was tempted to answer, "That charity begins at home", but Mavis Tyndall would take it as heresy, and Miss Havelock who, as Rose was aware, put first whatever suited her book at the time would make a platform of it. And Victorine, from cussedness, would call it misanthropy or prejudice—or politics if she wanted a row.

"I'm thinking of what we owe to Mr Cade, to the community as a whole, and to the church itself. Because that doesn't sound so—" Rose smiled faintly—"so human as Mrs Peachey, I'm wondering if we ought not to think of it all the more."

"Rose—ladies—I'm not to be thought of at all. The community, yes, the church, yes, but there's nothing owing to me." Cade looked into each face as Mavis Tyndall had done and with something of the same appeal. "It's I who owe everything—"

"If you do," said Rose, "a disgruntled congregation won't pay for it."

She saw the unwisdom of that at once but was too irritated to be sorry for him and turned to the others. "I'm not going to swap priorities, but I think you'll agree we do owe Mr

Cade adequate conditions of worship. True, the boilers will have to be replaced, but we must hope for help from parish funds for that. What I'm asking—and believe me, I'd like the answer to be 'yes', I'm open to conviction, I'd like nothing better than for you to convince me—is, do we have the right to beg or borrow a single penny to pay for the hassocks while we have money which was intended for just such a contingency?''

Victorine said, "Was our Hilda explicit about that?''

Rose picked up her minute book. "The wording of the bequest was as follows: 'I bequeath the monies accruing, that is, the interest payable quarterly on the aforenamed stock and holdings, to be used for the help and benefit of our church of St John's-on-the-Green and for those of its parishioners who shall be considered in want and worthy and likely to profit by such benefit. . . ' ''

"Well?''

"She put the church first.''

"That's just a convenient wording.''

Rose dropped her book with a cards-on-the-table gesture. "Frankly, I'm not sure. I can't help thinking that in this case Hilda might have wanted the church to have priority.''

"In Mrs Peachey's case,'' said Victorine.

It was odd that battle should come from this quarter, the last Rose would have armed against, supposing she had intended to arm. It meant that a battle was being sought with one who did not want to fight, on grounds which did not exist, by someone who didn't give a fig for them anyway.

Mavis Tyndall cried out, "Mrs Antrobus, why did you form a committee? Why did you ask us to decide when you'd already made up your mind?''

Rose leaned across and took both her hands. "My dear Mavis, didn't I just say that I'm open to conviction? That I'd be happy to be convinced? I formed a committee because I wanted advice and opinions other than my own and because this is only the first of many such sums which we shall be able to help people with. And I asked the Committee to decide because you yourself proposed Mrs Peachey as a beneficiary. You were at liberty to do so and so was

34

any other member of the Committee who knew of a deserving case."

"But if we're to be over-ruled—"

"You can't be over-ruled," Rose pointed out, patiently, "until you're in the minority."

"We can't be blamed," said Miss Havelock, majestically rising, "for not thinking alike, but it's a pity we had no margin to differ."

"That's hardly my fault—" began Rose, but Mrs Choules was talking.

"I can't fancy that family somehow. Not after what the man did. He put one of that poor woman's eyes out, you know. He beat her breasts to pulp and cracked her ribs, then he dirtied on her—you know, relieved himself all over her while she lay on the ground. Of course you can't blame the kiddies for any of that, but I'm funny that way, over-sensitive, I suppose. I just can't fancy any of them."

There was a bad silence. Everything that the abominable Mrs Choules had said went on sinking and sinking into it. Rose wanted to talk loudly, switch on music, run water, cover it up somehow. She felt sick. Something had been started which was not as fair as a fight, and the weapon was being used by Mrs Choules—not Victorine—as if it were versatile and cunning enough to go equally well into the hands of friends. Rose panicked. Not friends! Must she own to Mrs Choules because Mrs Choules had come to her, Rose's, conclusion? The way she had come?

Cade sat among them and it would have been helpful if he had not done it so thoroughly, if he could have risen a little above them, just by virtue of being male. Instead, he used his parson's status to lower himself to their level and he sat there with this fatuity, this oppressive women's burden of thinking with their skins, carrying it to God with all the other burdens he took upon himself.

Mavis Tyndall was as pale as she had been red before and seemed, now that there was a lot she might justifiably have said, to be beyond saying it. Victorine looked peaceable, more than she had done for a long time.

Miss Havelock had that air of disembarrassing herself.

Yet why should she? She was as much to blame as any of them, if blame could get into a gathering so well-intentioned.

"I'm sorry, Mrs Antrobus, as I said, I have another appointment. If you call any further meetings no doubt you'll get into touch."

Rose went to the door with her. There *was* blame and it was Rose's only in so far as she had convened them. She had herself, in innocence, located the moment, the lapse, whatever it was, under her own roof.

"Perhaps in a fortnight's time—we must reach a decision."

"Unless there are new facts to go upon, I shall not need to reconsider mine."

Miss Havelock stepped into the afternoon. Her black moiré shoulders disclaimed the spring sunlight. It flaked off them as it might off the hide of a sea beast.

After that the meeting broke up and the other ladies went, except Victorine, who poured herself another cup of tea. The last thing Rose wanted just then was a mental game of tag.

Cade, too, was put out by Victorine's remaining. He stood banging at the side-pockets of his jacket—his way of checking that his pipe was safely stowed and of hinting that he was about to leave.

"I'm staying till four-thirty," Victorine told him. "It will save hanging about in town—I have a hairdressing appointment at five."

"It doesn't matter—I mean—" He frowned at himself. "I must be off, anyway."

"Will you come Tuesday fortnight?" asked Rose.

"I have a deacons' meeting that afternoon."

"What can you do in a fortnight that you couldn't do today?" said Victorine.

"I may think of something between now and then."

"I could postpone my deacons."

"There's no point, Eric. If you won't vote, why come to be squabbled over?"

He stopped banging his pockets and held his hands over

36

them like a man who realises he has lost something. "I thought you were with me over this, I thought you understood my position, Rose, you of all people."

"Why 'of all people'? I can be as unreasonable as anyone else." Rose lay back in her chair and closed her eyes. It was quite something not to see the circle of faces, such a small circle, but they had tired her out.

Victorine asked Cade, "Was it true what Mrs Choules said Peachey did to that woman?"

"Yes. I went to see her."

Rose opened her eyes. "You did what?"

"And Denis Peachey." He bowed his head. "She was paralysed from the waist down."

"You knew that? All the time?"

"I went again after she came out of hospital. There's a chance the paralysis will be cured. It was largely due to shock. She isn't a young woman and she was, of course, terribly shocked."

"You said nothing about this at the meeting!"

"Why should I?"

Rose saw him carrying this burden, a real burden this time, of human misery. Carrying it—why? It was being carried already and he couldn't take one grain off anyone else's back. She wondered, did he pick it up now and then or did he cling on to it all the time?

"Why should I?" repeated Cade. "It had no bearing on what we were discussing."

"No bearing!" She had stopped to get breath. Then she saw their surprise and in Cade's face the beginning of dismay.

Instinctively she closed her eyes again. She had shown them something personal and private, something they had no business to see. She could not deny it and she need not apologise for it any more than for the mole on her neck. What disgusted her was that these two, Victorine and Cade, would not differentiate between what they saw in Mrs Choules and what they saw in her.

"No," she said blankly, "no bearing."

She kept her eyes shut against them, knowing by their

37

silence that they were not convinced. They had something now to suspect her of, a bag of reasons, Mrs Choules' mixed bag.

"You look tired, Rose."

"Who would have thought there'd be so much mischief in trying to get some new hassocks?"

"Mischief—" said Cade, "if you call it that—is what I tried to prevent."

"I do call it that and you couldn't prevent it. It was an epidemic. One of them came with it and the others caught it off her. Except Mavis Tyndall—she meant well."

"Was I the one," said Victorine, "who came with mischief?"

"You were the only one who made a game of the whole thing."

"But I really want Mrs Peachey to get the money. I want her to feel that life isn't passing her by entirely and if new saucepans can do that I think she should have them." She even smiled, nowadays, with the other side of her face. "Though it's a case of the blind leading the blind—little Tyndall, who thinks she knows, leading me who hopes she does."

Cade, who had been moving about, jibbing at something, let it erupt with that naïvety which, in a man of God, was excused and indeed expected, but which Cade himself had not needed to acquire. "Rose, we must drop it—the church's claim, I mean. I should not have allowed it to go forward—"

"You could hardly have prevented it," said Rose. "And I certainly can't withdraw now."

"Not if I ask you as a personal favour?"

"You have no right to ask and I should have to refuse because, as I said before, it's culpable when a parish of this size and importance has such a poorly furnished church."

"We could raise the money—"

"There's a limit to money-raisers and I think we've reached it. We're committed to asking for money for everything from hunger in Asia to the unmarried mothers at Poll Hill. Should we ask for more? When this is just the sort of

38

thing Hilda intended the fund for? And what you're hoping it will do for Mrs Peachey is so unlikely—it's unrealistic and I'm not even sure it's just."

"Mrs Peachey's white," said Victorine, "but she's not tidy."

Rose sat up. She had had enough, more than anyone in her position need patiently endure. These two, Victorine and Cade, had piled on their straws, and now she was ready, though not to break.

"Vee, you came to make mischief and you've made it. I don't know why. Whether you're sick in your mind or your body, I don't think it matters. It can't excuse your attitude. And I shan't apologise to you, Eric. You fret about keeping in with God and the neighbours and you're not sure which is the most important. When you've made up your mind perhaps we'll get somewhere. Between now and Tuesday fortnight I suggest you both re-examine your motives and prepare to state them as frankly as Mrs Choules did."

Victorine was swallowing and relishing the smoke of her cigarette. "Which do you think is the more important, her frankness or her motives?"

Cade, pink and most raw where the hair backed across his scalp, slapped at his pockets and blundered to the door. "Excuse me, I must be off." He was gone, taking the hurt air with him.

"He can't forgive you," said Victorine, "but he'll keep trying."

Ted Antrobus had habits which he took care of and kept for years. It disturbed him if any of them were broken. Sometimes he was disturbed in anticipation. When he came home he could not relax until a ritual was complete, it was part of the journey and he did not arrive until then.

When he did relax he was a different person and his fellow-commuters were struck by the discrepancy between the man they travelled with and the man they met on the golf-course and in the vicinity of his home. On the train he was a loud and frequent talker. He was considered an extensive man, ready to play poker or talk usefully about any of the subjects that normally came up.

At home he was quiet, lacking conviction, his opinions had to be pulled out of him. He had a way of gazing past people while he spoke and it made him appear preoccupied and distant. He wore bulky tweeds like a landowner. The only land he had the remotest interest in had eighteen holes and a club-house. His game was poor, but he disdained to work at it. To Rose he said that he played because it gave him somewhere to walk to.

Rose did not hear the sharp stories on the train, but if she had she would have recognised that he was getting into gear, she understood that at home he was not by any means fully extended.

She would not have cared for him to be. When she had occasion to be in the company of his wound-up self she experienced a faint, persistent disquiet. Years ago she attributed it to anxiety that she would not be able to keep up with him. He was so much the centre of things, quite a dynamo, and she still told people, 'Ted's a dynamo when he's working'. But she knew now that her fears of not being quite in his class were justified. His class, his working class, was a peg lower than her own. It had been a shock finding out and she had even thought how she might tone him down—a little less panache, a little more reticence, not so much club camaraderie. Thank God she had never tried it. She soon realised that if she was slightly ashamed of her husband there was nothing to be done except never to let him or anyone else see it.

He had worked out for himself what he could most usefully and profitably be, and this was his interpretation of it. For practical purposes it was successful and there was no reason why he should be badgered to adjust it, even if he could, by a hairsbreadth here and there. Rose did not consider her own taste sufficient reason, suspecting that it was astringent and too particular. Easy to take was what Ted had thought it necessary to be, and was able to be, at the drop of a hat, for business and potentially business purposes.

His job and its milieu did advance one type of personality

which he was able to reproduce exactly. He was London and Continental Manager for a car-hire firm. He had cut himself into the job: had he decided to be a solicitor or a dentist he could as faithfully have cut himself into theirs. Rose would have preferred that. But neither profession could have paid him better than the car-hire business unless he had been exceptionally successful. Rose concluded he was wise not to attempt what he might not achieve. It was not that which she had against him. If she had anything, it was simply that between being an authentic businessman and resting from it, he had little time to be himself.

It would be ironic if anyone with two personalities should not be found in either. Rose preferred to think of them as the opposite ends of one personality, with Ted Antrobus, real, midway between. She had settled contentedly enough for the quiet end, the homecoming man who said little and whom she could therefore assume thought along her own lines.

She ministered to his habits wherever it was required of her and in the course of time they had come to formulate and fix habits of her own, so that each day, however untidily it might turn out, had a ritual to begin and end with.

Rose was glad of that on the day of the meeting. More than most people she disliked things not going to plan and she particularly disliked how they had not gone on this occasion. The ladies had proved to be a backward people, unobjective, bound up in themselves to an unhealthy degree, and Victorine Gregory, of course, was more than out of sorts.

The impression was of something residual and feminine which had no business on a committee. Rose did not like even to have it in the house. She opened windows and let in the sharp rainy air, she herself walked round the garden to freshen up. She would have liked to wipe out the afternoon and make another start. She felt that she should have handled the meeting better: she should, in fact, have handled it. It had gone agley because Mrs Peachey's was a redolent case. Rose had not known how redolent, nor reckoned how the mixture of violence, sex and Mavis Tyndall's mawkishness would operate. She certainly had not reckoned—how could she?—its effect on a mind as unbalanced as Victorine Gregory's. It had brought out the worst in her at a time when the worst was sillier and more contrary than usual.

Rose said something of the sort to Ted Antrobus that evening after he had changed out of his City clothes, after he had appeared to choose the sweet black sherry he invariably drank before dinner, first offering it to her and she, as always, had preferred a dry Martini, after he had closed his eyes for ten minutes, unwinding, with the empty glass held on his knee and in that spell which was reserved for broaching discussion of her affairs or a simple brief comment on her day.

Antrobus kept himself informed about Rose's activities. He knew the days of her meetings and the names of the committees she served on. He retained a potted history of the various protagonists. It was a kind of privileged after-hours extension of his methodical business mind.

"How did the Self-Help Committee meeting go?"

"It didn't," said Rose, and told him about Victorine. "I suspect she's going through a difficult time."

"Oh?"

"She's at an awkward age," Rose said delicately, "and she's always inclined to be mischievous in a silly, though harmless way. Now I'm afraid there's quite a bit of harm in it."

"To you?"

"To everyone. Of course she'll harm herself most of all."

"Of course."

"It's a period of maladjustment which certainly doesn't fit her for public life."

"Nor for private."

"I don't want to be unkind, but I think she's poisoned at the source. Physically, I mean. One shouldn't minimise the effects of the over- or under-stimulation even of glands—"

"There's no danger of that," said Antrobus, "once it's been observed by the Club."

"The Club? The Golf Club? Vee's not a member."

"Sam Swanzy is."

"Has he been talking about her?"

"I doubt it. Not if they are—" he looked absently over Rose's shoulder—"having fun together."

"Sam Swanzy? Vee?" Rose, incredulous, started to smile. "Oh, surely not!" And was at once convinced. "She couldn't!" Her disgust at its outset was less than righteous. "Sam Swanzy of all people!"

"Fun, anyway, for him."

"I really can't credit it. He's repulsive, he's—" Rose shuddered—"raw. I'm always afraid he's going to leave meaty marks wherever he touches." She got up. She could not sit there with Antrobus as a background to what she might think. She was shocked and every minute the shock deepened, she didn't know where it would end. "Of course if she's got that on her conscience it's bound to be warped. Why didn't you tell me before? You knew I was going to invite her to join the Committee."

"It was only Club gossip."

"You should have told me! She is a friend of mine—"

"I didn't believe it."

"And now you do?"

"I see no reason to. But in the circumstances you should perhaps bear it in mind."

She should of course do no more. But she did not seem to be in any mind so much as a flux. It would be a while before she could support the knowledge, suspicion, doubt, proviso—whatever it was.

"Why didn't Sue Betts tell me?"

"She may not have heard it. Gossip has to filter and there's a story to go with it that's not been made fit for ladies yet."

"Do you know, I'm inclined to believe it. It's what she would do, out of perversity. Anyone else wanting—" Rose picked it up with tongs—"anything like that, would at least choose someone presentable. Vee would go to the other extreme, the way she could do most damage to everyone, herself included."

She had done appreciable damage to Rose: not that Rose had a superfine opinion of Victorine, but she had given her

43

credit for a reserve of decency, even at her climacteric. However, it need not have disturbed her and she was at a loss to know why it seemed to take the lid off something.

"It confirms what I was saying. She's thoroughly unbalanced."

Mentally and physically. Wanting Sam Swanzy's hands on her, wanting his meaty body, his glistening lips, his tongue—Rose felt sick. She turned her face to the wall, shamed as if she and all womankind were of the same dirty feather. "That sort of thing makes me ill."

Antrobus was looking through his empty sherry glass. "This glass isn't true at the base, it slightly distorts." When she made no comment he added, "You have no doubt what sort of thing it is?"

"Have you?"

"I?" He seemed surprised to be asked. "You know her better than I do."

"I didn't know she had it in her, but since she has it was her duty not to let it out. We do wrong to excuse so much. There used to be something else besides sickness and health, there used to be sin, and if it doesn't exist any more we don't need priests or policemen, we only need doctors."

"Surgeons," said Antrobus, examining the weave of his cuff through the glass, "to cut out the bad parts."

"Vee is as capable as I am of choosing right from wrong. The only sickness," Rose said sharply, "was in the choice she had to make."

"It wouldn't do for us all to like the same things."

"That's not funny." He was unsmiling and she said bitterly, "No doubt it was mixed up with her reason for blocking me."

It was her experience that people beyond the pale, particularly if they had put themselves there, could not forgive those inside it. They had no wish to get back, they simply wanted to deny the pale's existence and show everyone as suspect. Hence Victorine's efforts to discredit.

Antrobus said gently, "What have you got against this Mrs Peachey?"

"Nothing. Why does everyone think I have? For Heaven's sake, she's in trouble enough."

"Enough."

Antrobus had a way of picking up and dropping other people's last words and Rose, though she knew the trick, cried, "I've never even seen her!"

There was no need for his silence to pique her: she knew that it came from acceptance rather than question. He had never dug into her motives and she suspected that he scratched the surface out of politeness and a sense of duty.

"The point I make, and I think it's valid, is that given a sympathetic, not to say a sentimental hearing, she might dramatise her situation. Mavis Tyndall is a good little thing, but far from objective. Mrs Peachey would spend the money and it wouldn't change anything. How could it? Forty pounds odd," said Rose, "when what she needs is a miracle."

"Perhaps you should see her."

"What good would it do? They've made up their minds and nothing I could say would change them."

Of late Rose had caught herself in the mirror thrusting up her chin as she spoke. She was afraid it was a nervous tick, out of keeping with anything she might have to say and she was trying to break it. "I'm not the parish visitor type—" Yes, she had just done it again, an uppish jerk, defensive and clumsy. If she looked like that everyone was going to think she had something to defend. "And I doubt if I could change my mind when I don't approve the idea in principle. It's unrealistic to think that money can give her moral courage. And insulting, especially when the money's so little."

Antrobus and Rose had long ago established a method of picking out only what they wanted of each other's thoughts and emotions. Sometimes something was not soon enough refused—as now, when there were the elements of a smile on his face. Rose took it that her motives, or what he made of them, amused him. Knowing that he would not trouble to make anything upset her.

"I thought Eric Cade was common-sensible. If there is

45

nothing else, one may expect a pastor to have both his feet on the ground. Surely?"

"On the ground," Antrobus agreed and put the sherry glass aside to show that he was ready for supper.

Rose lifted her chin again. "I don't expect to have to chase to God after him."

PART TWO

It's no coincidence that I think of Solange now: I don't for months at a time, then something or someone will remind me.

She's been coming on, every day a little more, and I don't need to be reminded now. Now she has so much relevance it is difficult not to think of her. I'm beginning to believe she can interpret for me. She's with me now as she was at Bonneval and Grieux, and more so because now she is in my mind and I can deny her nothing, forbid her nothing. *In absentiâ* she has the entrée of a ghost and the influence of a god, in the flesh she was most fallible.

She is a case in point. In point of this, which I can't put a name to. There may be a technical term for it, something psychological, something German, something *angst*. It's a question and not a new one. I think I've been answering it all my life.

And Solange has been my answer since the day, the communion day at Bonneval. I was twelve years old, I wouldn't be likely to have asked the question before then. Solange may have helped to pose it. She and all that she implied may be not just a case in point but a microcosm. One must particularise—I must. If I'm to answer and be done with this question which presents itself to me from all sides I must take as I find and I can only hope to find in my own past experience. It's better than any I could get now by asking other people. I must prove, or fail to, by what I know, not by what I'm told.

I am taking a case in point—I want to be secure about that from the outset. Because it is possible to look at a drop of something and assume it to be tap-water and blame the entire plumbing system on it, and then have it turn out to be a drop of lemonade or turpentine or plasma.

I know that Solange was human, a normal human being.

49

I don't go so far as to say that the other sort, if they exist, are *in*human. If they exist.

Holiness won't save anyone. I learned that early, it was perhaps the first difficult thing I did learn. Not that I was ever religious, I had just been brought up to three of everything: earth where we lived and sinned in some degree, hell where we went if the degree was excessive and heaven where there was God and unrelieved good and where we should all end up singing. To me at twelve years old that was the Establishment, I was content with it and supposed everyone was.

Remembering Bonneval is like turning back the pages of a book and re-reading, even to what was said, and how, and why. I can't guarantee the accuracy of conversations, I haven't the gift for total recall, but I do seem to have registered their impact.

Most of the time I was shocked: what happened at Bonneval unmade me, I had afterwards to do some work on myself. Then at Grieux, in Switzerland, where I was at school, the whole thing happened again, only worse because I was older and had to come down to earth and it seemed that the earth wasn't going to support me either.

I wonder how I would have turned out if there had been no Bonneval and no Grieux. Perhaps no differently to all intents and purposes other than my own. I would still have married Ted Antrobus, though for reasons which must have been the wrong ones. Because we do see what we need to in people. What I needed to see in Ted happened actually to be there.

I may have been lucky too in what I saw in Solange. If I really did see in her that special element, power, quirk, streak, quality—or lack of it—that I can see now the world over. Or did I only need to see and needing, supplied it? One can only supply what already exists and only *where* it doesn't exist. But surely if anyone ever had it, Solange Marigny did.

She was my pen-friend. Before we met I used to suppose her blonde and soft and dressed in pink. I thought her name had a squashy sound. She wrote to me in English and I had to reply in French. I still have some of her letters. They are very correct, I thought them dull.

'We go to the Bois de Boulogne which is in Paris and on Sundays full of tradesmen.' 'The weather has been bad. It has rained since Easter every day. Madame Molette, our doorkeeper, has a glass eye which presages the weather. When it will rain the eye is green, when it will be fine the eye is yellow. When we have storm she removes it because of the lightning.'

One letter, I remember, my father found illuminating. Perhaps it was one in which she wrote: 'We are not permitted to go to the Parc Parangon. My mother says we will understand presently. It is not a pretty place, there are no flowers, they have naturally been all crushed.'

He said, "That girl's a minx," and when I asked why, he said all French females were minxes, it was the national character.

He was dubious about letting me go to stay with the Marignys. But Mother was adamant, she admired all things Continental.

I was an outright English child, too keen on games, dainty as a bear, with an undiscriminating appetite for what I was sure was going to be an appetising world. I had no fear and no finesse. I had everything to learn and I was insulated against learning it. No doubt what my mother intended I should acquire in France was not so much a polish as some cracks in the glaze. She wasn't to know they would be splits, nor that they would reach down to the foundations.

The Marignys were comfortably off. Solange's father was a lawyer and was called 'Maître'. They had a flat in Paris and what Solange called a 'domaine' in the country. Bonneval was just south of Bordeaux, in the wine country, that part of France which once was Aquitaine. When the letter came from Madame Marigny to my mother inviting me to spend the summer holidays with Solange I didn't want to go. There were tennis finals in July, I was in the first eleven of the local ladies' cricket team and we had plenty of fixtures. But cricket wasn't of the slightest concern to my mother, she disapproved of my playing because it was a man's game

51

and she thought the hard balls dangerous. And so my father, when he raised objection to my going abroad, was accused of encouraging me to be a hoyden, a 'hermaphrodite' my mother called it.

"I will not have Rose becoming one of those with bosoms and no gender," I heard her say. "She needs to be taught her sex and no one can give her better grounding than the French."

My father tried to be sceptical about my having sex at twelve years old, but Mother said I'd been born with it and must learn to use it or leave it alone—but no daughter of hers was going to leave it alone.

So in the summer of 1927 I went to Bonneval. I was put in the charge of a stewardess on the boat to Calais. As it was a rough crossing she was fully occupied and I was left to myself.

I found that I was a good sailor and ate an enormous lunch. Afterwards I went up on deck where there were sick people flattened like wet flies by the roaring wind, putting their faith, I suppose, in fresh air however brutal. No one had heart or lungs enough to speak to me except a woman who strode about talking to everyone. She was not seasick and thought it proved the purity of her liver. She wasn't impressed with mine because she maintained I hadn't had time to spoil it. Whenever she passed she shouted, "Keep your liver clean!" and if I have to think of liver now I can smell wet iron and salt and feel the boat struggling in mid-air like a bird in the hand. Just before we docked, this woman slipped and cracked her skull on the deck. She was carried below on a stretcher.

I was a believer in justice, though not morbidly and as a *status quo* rather than a golden or sacred mean. Pride before a fall, good after bad, right after wrong seemed to me ordered as day after night. I had no sympathy with the liver woman, I considered she had been served right for being a fool and for boasting and I went ashore like a lion—the chosen, the fittest survivor among all the sorry voyagers.

Monsieur Marigny, who had business in Calais, was to meet me off the boat and take me to Bonneval. I had no idea what to expect, but he apparently was not in doubt about me. As soon as I stepped off the gangplank he was at my side, a small vivid man with a badly scarred and eroded face. He was pale, his hair and moustache were jetty black and I always saw him in black clothes, yet there was a reptilian brilliance about him. It could only have come from within, from something suppressed and inimical. I have not forgotten him: he was the first intimation I had that I was going somewhere completely and fundamentally foreign.

He said, "M'oiselle," bowing slightly. "Je m'appelle Quentin Marigny. Soyez la bienvenue."

I had the shell I was born with and which my slice of life had merely established. I felt no more than momentarily abashed, I was able to look away from anything that promised to be without profit and three-quarters forget it. I suppose that's what I did with Maître Marigny at our first meeting because of the long train journey to Paris and the still longer one from Paris to Bonneval he remains as a faint discomfiture, a cold-finger accompaniment. He probably wished it so, he had no interest in me except as a parcel for delivery.

There was one encounter between us just after the train left Calais. I got up from my seat to go along the corridor and Maître Marigny said, "Mademoiselle?"

That did stump me. While I was trying to formulate in French something slightly left of an unmistakable centre he leaned forward and tapped the seat beside me. "Asseyez-vous, s'il vous plaît."

"I want to go along the corridor."

"Comment?"

"To wash my hands."

He looked at me with brows raised, then he said, "Go," and sat back in his corner. He took no further notice of me until we got to Paris. It was as if I had demonstrated my normality and could be allowed the latitude of a trained dog.

I got tired travelling all day and all night and slept for most of the journey from Paris. Maître Marigny sat under his individual light reading a sheaf of papers and occasionally writing on them. He started before the train drew out of Austerlitz and he was still at it when we reached Bordeaux.

We had to change to a branch line, a little rusty train with a cow-catcher and slat seats like we had at home on the trams. It took us through miles of what I later learned were vineyards. It was very hot, the carriages and everything in them were doused with white dust, Maître Marigny was smoking terrible brown cigarettes and it felt as if every bit of France I had travelled over had been pushed down my throat. I looked longingly at the rivers we passed, lacquered black or running thin over stones the colour of pigeons. Every farm with its brown-speckled pantiles and every cow made me think of cold milk—I longed for a glass of ice-cold milk.

The train stopped every few minutes and people got in and out, women with frizzy hair and huge loaded baskets like the baker's roundsman carried at home, and men with no socks and dirty canvas shoes. Some of them wore wide straw hats and their clothes were splashed with a beautiful poignant blue. Everyone smelled terrible, I began to feel dazed. They seemed to know Maître Marigny and they all spoke to him. Sometimes he grunted, more often he briefly relaxed the scars on his face by way of acknowledgment.

It was noon when we reached Bonneval. By then I had been travelling for twenty-eight hours, I was sick and tired and hot and cross and the sweat was running down the backs of my knees. I just dropped out of the train, leaving Maître Marigny to deal with every scrap of luggage. He called a porter and the porter and people still in the carriage got my bags and parcels out between them while the train waited, sinking us in clouds of steam. I appreciated that Maître Marigny was a different proposition from my father who personally escorted every piece of luggage out of trains and always got back in at the risk of being carried on, to make sure that everything down to the last discarded paper bag stayed with us. It nettled me that anyone could be so absolutely undiminished by all that heat and noise. He was as crisp and accurate and obscurely brilliant as he had been at

Calais, the dust that was everywhere, even between my teeth, had not settled on him. I think I concluded then and there that Solange's father was mineral whereas on the whole the race of adults were vegetable.

I can remember the heat of that first day at Bonneval. When the train had gone, and the steam, it was apparent that what was the matter was the sun. It had an emulsifying effect, the metal railway lines and the bones of my body were ready to leak away together but the air had thickened, the air had to be supported.

A car waited outside the station. Beside it stood two children. Maître Marigny stooped to allow each of them to kiss him on either side of his cigarette. Then he turned to me.

"Permettez-moi de vous présenter Valentin, mon fils, et Solange, ma fille."

The girl shook me by the hand. I believe she said she was happy to make my acquaintance as if, I thought, I was going again after tea. The boy stooped and touched my knuckles with his lips. I felt ridiculous and he was obviously unaware that he looked it. He was very thin, all angle and bone, outgrowing his skin as well as his clothes. He wore a sort of Norfolk suit, I remember. It was too small and his wrists and legs sprouted, so did his neck. He was then, and always I believe, what my grandmother would have called a 'poor tool'.

Solange made little impression on me at first sight. I saw that she was dark and slender where I had anticipated someone fattish and fair, but I didn't look at her much, I was inclined to sulk because these people weren't going to understand me.

Château de Bonneval was the next disturbance. We drove through a village, just a collection of cracked and shuttered shells, and a church, then along an unmade road that climbed through fields of vines to a bleached common ringed with mauve flowers. Solange, who was sitting opposite, said politely, "Voici le château". I looked, and there it was, on a terraced hill with a sort of tumult of green woods at its feet. Ordinarily I would have been enchanted and later on

I was, but that first glimpse upset me. I got angry with Solange for not preparing me. She had written of 'our house in the country' and my father had maintained that French people called anything a 'château'.

"We're the same" he'd said, "putting 'Ivanhoe' and 'Windsor' and 'Harlech' on every front-yard gate." The obvious interpretation, that it really was a château with candle-snuffer towers and arched windows and a front door that a coach could drive through, had never occurred to us. I came to it unapprised from the mustard villas of South London.

Buckingham and the Crystal Palaces were monuments, cathedrals were religion: I discounted them, and Paddington Station, as geographical rather than designed and had supposed that our new baroque cinema, the Otranto, was the most I could except to take architecturally.

From the vision floating in that hot nacreous light out of the pages of Hans Andersen and the Rose Fairy Book, I looked at the Marignys. I had grown out of this sort of thing and so, I considered, should they have done. They had no right to live in such a place, but it was the sort of far-fetched foreign thing they would do and might have been excused— like the Japanese fancy for living in paper houses—so long as they hadn't brought me into it. A fine fool I should look, and feel, in a place like that, a fish out of water, a bird out of air.

My tennis-racquet was on the floor of the car at my feet. I have large feet and Mother used to make me wear broad shoes to give me room to grow. Beside my tongued leather brogues which looked pretty stylish at home, I saw Solange's bare foot in the same sort of canvas slipper that the men on the train were wearing. The same sort of dirt was on it too, a patina of dust grained into the cloth and into her brown ankle. The bone was polished and slaty with it. How foreign, I wondered in disgust, was it allowable for these people to be?

As the car choked up the hill to the Château, Maître Marigny spoke to me for about the third time since we had left Calais. It was quite an 'histoire' for him. He told me, I

56

think, because I never could follow his French very well, that in the seventeenth century Château de Bonneval was the home of the poet and essayist, Edouard Brindille, famous for his intrigues as well as his writings. He was murdered at the Château by a lady of quality whom he had betrayed. She pushed a hat-pin into his ear.

"Vous voyez donc que Bonneval est un château très intéressant, très historique et très romantique," concluded Maître Marigny.

I said, "Evidemment," and he looked at me as if I'd made a rude noise.

I expected the Marignys to put on airs at living in a place like that, but I soon found that their airs had nothing to do with the Château. They took that for granted.

There was none the less a sort of collective air which, although they had quite different personalities, was peculiar to all of them and to the place. It was indigenous perhaps, bred up out of that country of vines and dust, parrot-green forests and bath-tub heat. An unsettling air—it unsettled me, I didn't feel safe, in a daily sense, with any of them. They were incalculable, and although I was too brash to calculate anyone, I wanted people to abide by my rough and ready reckoning of them. The Marignys were slippery but not deceitful. They did not hide what they were, it was up to the beholder to make it out. I never could, I beheld it in all of them, at times as uncalled for and disquieting as the lightning that always seemed to be blinking like a white eyelid at the back of the sky.

The Château didn't impress me so much on the inside. The entrance hall was grand enough in a medieval way: it had a stone floor and rather chewed wooden roof-beams and a great cowled fireplace with one of Edouard Brindille's *bon mots* carved above it. There were swords and daggers on the walls but not the hat-pin that had killed him. The rooms downstairs were darkened by the Spanish chestnut trees outside the windows and by the panelling which sometimes continued over the ceiling like a box. There was a library, that was enormous too, with a ladder to get to the top-most shelves, and as I dislike the smell of old books it was noisome. The family camped out in a corner for after-dinner coffee.

From upstairs there was a view across miles of vines, meadows and forest. The walls of the principal rooms were covered with patterned fabrics. Solange told me that her great-grandmother had done it when material was cheaper than wallpaper. There were three storeys to the Château. I liked the rooms inside the towers, they were circular and too small to lie down in and their slit windows were the only ones without shutters.

Apart from the addition of basket chairs, stuffed stools and woollen rugs, the Marignys didn't appear to have changed the furniture much since Solange's great-grand-mother's time. I thought it all ugly and shabby, though now I appreciate that they must have had a lot of good things, real antiques—chiffoniers and escritoires and those slender bow-fronted chairs, massive beds and court cupboards that you could get into, marquetry tables, buhl clocks—that sort of thing. There were even some tapestries which could have been Gobelin. None of it was looked after, whatever pride the Marignys had, it wasn't pride of possession.

Solange told me, that first day, that the Château belonged to her mother. It had been in that side of the family for over a hundred years but wasn't likely to remain so much longer. I gathered it was something of a white elephant, a white mammoth, costly to run and much in need of repair. The vines had been sold and the farms. There was only the forest now, and what little money could be made out of the timber went to pay the bailiff who was unscrupulous and lazy. Solange told me this politely since I had asked questions, but indifferently. She was with me in my room while I unpacked and was more interested in my clothes than any-thing else. I began to feel scandalised, from being angry with her because I expected her to put on airs I switched to being indignant because she didn't. Anyone who had a place like this, I reasoned, ought to regard it as their duty to keep it for their children and their children's children. English people did, I said, they starved in drawing-rooms rather than let their ancestral homes out of the family. I was mixed up there, but from the beginning Solange had a knack of making me righteous, however misinformed. She just shrugged and smiled, I remember, and tried on my dressing-gown.

I didn't reach her then, or ever, but it was a long time before I gave up trying. I couldn't get used to living on anyone's periphery although that was as far as I got with any of the Marignys. For such a discrepant group they were strangely united. It was as if their differences kept them together. They relied on each other for the essential grit in their lives: it was the only thing, I sometimes thought, that was essential to them. They loved to differ and they aired their differences without acrimony, a point of interest more than honour. They didn't seem to go in for deep committed things like honour, they had plenty of opinions, but I never was sure what they believed in.

Madame Marigny was the most unaccountable. Her husband I placed, or rather wrote off, under his profession: I allowed only for law in a lawyer, medicine in a doctor and teeth in a dentist. Madame Marigny, although French, was a mother and should have known her place. Had she stayed in it I could have allowed and appreciated a few foreign quirks.

Madame Marigny didn't stay anywhere, even while we were at meals she would get up and wander round the table. This I considered inexcusable since she had the gall to supervise her children's manners. One moment she was all she ought to be, she was 'Maman' and the household goddess: the next she was chattering and gesturing and grimacing like mad—literally like, no-one sane could have swallowed so much air. Or she would move away, stiffly, and because she had blue bulbous eyes and pink bulbous cheeks and puffs of flaxen hair she looked like a badly-jointed doll. Sometimes she ran. If, for reasons known only to herself, she needed to get away quicker, she picked up her skirts and flashed out of the room. Once I saw her, while they were having an evening party, run like that across the moonlit terrace and into the garden and come back a minute later looking as if she'd caught and eaten something. Sometimes she just beat the air with her hands. Sometimes she laughed, quietly and glitteringly—she had gold fillings in her teeth—and that was the only time I really minded her.

Valentin favoured his mother in looks. He had the same overshot eyes and boiled yellow hair. He was growing too fast and the sun which darkened other boys fetched him up a raw, painful red. He was said to be lazy, the family said so without condemnation, as they would say that the soil was chalk, but later on Maître Marigny, looking for something specific to say of his son, could find only that and made it a crime.

I didn't understand Valentin any better than the others, but I liked him better. I thought him preoccupied rather than lazy, he was trying to use his mind. The time he spent lying on the grass and dribbling a ball about the garden was devoted to questions which most people didn't ask. He asked them of me, he probably hoped that a foreigner could give him a new slant. I couldn't, of course. He either put his questions badly in English or too well in French and I wouldn't even try to get the substance. They were, I thought, the sort of presumptuous nonsense God might answer with a thunderbolt.

Céline, the youngest, was called Chelle. She was nine years old and she was the practical one. She was plain in a monkeyish way, dark and small like her father but without his suppressed brilliance. She sometimes twinkled with private glee and darted out her tongue when she laughed. I felt uncomfortable in her presence. She was so quick and I mistrusted speed in people, but I couldn't snub her as I might an English child of her age because she pretended not to understand either my French or my English.

Finally there was Solange, and I have left her until last in the hope, even now, that she might clarify against my impressions of her family. I want to be fair, to see her in the round. It will be difficult because in remembering what she was I can't put out of my mind what she became. What we both became. Impartial, perhaps I can be in one sense, since I was never sure what I felt for Solange. I am still not sure: for anything that I liked about her I can remember something that I disliked. There's no bias but there may be some myopia—she's so much a part of the furniture of my mind I shan't see for looking.

She was pretty, and being at that time part child, part woman gave to her looks an ideal quality. We'd all like to be fixed about then, with a foot in both worlds. She had fine dark hair and a strong luminous pallor. She was very slender, almost spun. I felt like a rough pony beside her. She weighed about two stone less than I did, yet I have seen her carrying Chelle with ease under one arm. She took everything easily, win or lose, good or bad. Hers was a protective polish and nothing could get a grip on her.

I resented that. Life hadn't gripped on me either, but I often had to try for what I wanted. Figuratively speaking, Solange didn't lift a finger.

She acted as a catalyst on me, inducing emotions I didn't recognise as my own. There was a lot of prejudice and prissiness—I was trying to supply what was lacking in Solange. I began as soon as we met, when I had no more than got wind of it. I went on prickling and puffing up until the last.

During those first days at Bonneval the physical and mental climate was as remote as darkest Africa from anything I had known. The heat confused me, I have always preferred to be temperate, and I got into a waiting frame of mind, waiting for the pressure to lift, to stop, to go back to normal. Tomorrow, I used to think, when it's cooler. . . It never was cooler, not that summer. In the mornings, early, there would be a semblance of it, patches under the chestnut trees that might be damp, the forest tented and dark, and a thin green sky without a sun. I was seldom awake so soon.

We children had breakfast—coffee and unbuttered bread—at nine o'clock in the kitchen. My father had told me that French bread was good but this was dark and slightly sour.

Breakfast was prepared by Madame Dubosque. She was a distant elderly relation of Maître Marigny, she and her husband stayed the year round at the Château. Everyone

61

called her Tin-Tin, but I didn't care. She was a formidable old woman, dressed all in black, with nicotine coloured hair and negroid lips that looked horribly as if they were puckered for a kiss. She had a clownish sense of humour. On my first morning I asked if I might have a boiled egg for breakfast. She flew at me, flapping her skirts and clucking like a hen and chased me round the kitchen. I was very much put out, but Solange and Valentin rocked with laughter.

"You might have warned me she was touched," I said bitterly afterwards.

"Comment?"

"Mad." I tapped my forehead. "Folle."

Solange said Madame Dubosque was not mad, she was very 'sage' but she liked to amuse herself. I thought, she shan't do it at my expense and thereafter dipped my bread in my coffee as the others did and ate it soggy. It seemed revolting, but I had to eat something, I was always hungry.

Maître and Madame Marigny seldom appeared before lunch, and Chelle breakfasted earlier than we did. She was 'affairé', they said. It puzzled me what affairs a child of nine could have. Perhaps she was studying for something. But I found out what Chelle's standing was with the family when an American student who was writing his thesis on Edouard Brindille was shown round the Château. Chelle kept running from room to room so that she was always there before him with a big edition of Brindille's works held prominently before her. That time I felt it was my turn to laugh.

But Valentin said seriously, "Chelle thinks it is good for business."

The staff at the Château was made up of old women with faces like brown crusts. I couldn't tell them apart, nor could I understand their accent. With Monsieur Dubosque I had some intelligible conversations because he insisted on talking to me in dumb show as if I was a deaf mute. He worked in the garden, sorting over bits of gravel or picking off leaves, and whenever I appeared he seemed to be seized with intense pity for me. He went to a lot of trouble to communicate: there we would be, I talking primer French very slowly, he gesturing, capering, stretching and bunching his empty

62

rubber jaws. I finally had to accept the fact that he thought I was mentally deficient, a cave-dweller and a heathen, doomed to extinction in the rush of progress. He worked hard to make me laugh. I can see him now, putting his hat on back to front and doing a soft-shoe shuffle in the gravel. He was the only person at the Château who was *concerned* with me, who put himself out for me and I appreciated it, whatever his reasons.

We children were left to ourselves, no one entertained or instructed us. I was glad, I didn't want to go looking at graves and old buildings. At the same time my conscience or conceit took exception to the fact that no one tried to show me anything.

"My parents will want to know what I've seen," I said to Solange. "I'll have to tell them I didn't."

"Didn't?"

"See cathedrals and tombs."

"You wish to?"

"Of course not. The point is, my parents expect me to see the historical stuff while I'm here and I'll have to write an essay for school."

"There are books."

"It's not the same thing. I'm supposed to see the places myself—"

"Who shall say you have not seen?"

"That would be lying—cheating."

Her trick of smiling things off was still new to me. She was twelve years old and so was I, yet she could smile and put into my head the notion that I had a long way to go to catch up with her. It was only a notion, but it was insufferable because I didn't realise then that the way she was going I neither wanted to nor could catch up with her.

"I'm not a liar," I said. "Even if you are."

She went on smiling. "Like George Washington?" and I thought, you see what it's worth, she has no respect for anyone and that's not advanced, that's retarded.

Solange may have mentioned this conversation to her mother because a few days afterwards she and I were sent into Bordeaux with Madame Dubosque who was going to

63

buy herself some new corsets, and that was the farthest we went from the Château.

Solange and I spent the days together, in the forest, in the garden or sometimes we lay like dogs on the cool marble floor in the library. Occasionally Valentin was with us, more often he mooched about by himself.

Chelle had no time for us. She was forever scurrying about being busy. Or a busybody—I couldn't take her seriously. Everyone else did. It was she who kept Madame Marigny's accounts for the timber transactions. In an old scullery they called the 'office' were parcels of yellow papers and bills on hooks and old calendars. The calendars hung all over the walls, the earliest one being for 1905. Chelle had found them in a cupboard and put them up, perhaps to give her some of the time she was so short of. Also on the wall was a map she had drawn of the land the family still owned. Even to me it looked a most competent affair, contour lines, buildings, tracks, streams were all drawn in—how accurately I don't know—and the varieties of trees were shaded in different colours. It was possible to see at once where fir predominated, or chestnut, oak, pine and beech. Felling in progress was shown by black markers on pins. Chelle sat at a roll-topped desk with a huge horn-backed ledger before her. In this she wrote spidery French figures, the sevens all crossed like fives and the ones tabbed like sevens, credit and debit columns fenced off in red and violet inks.

Chelle was so sure of herself and everyone else was so sure that I refused to be. I asked Solange, "Why does your mother let Chelle play about like that?" Solange said Chelle wasn't playing, she was working and Madame Marigny was glad to have someone to do her additions.

"She ought to be pushing her dolls' pram!"

"Pourquoi tu te mets en colère?"

"I'm not angry! I just think it's mad to trust a kid her age—"

Solange went behind me and wrapped both my plaits round my neck. I thought she said in French something about me never being as old as Chelle, it was the sort of thing she would say.

Discovering a tennis-court in the Château grounds was a great thrill to me, although I was horrified at the state it was in. Weeds had cracked it, the net had never been wound in and fell apart like a cobweb, the posts were rotten and there weren't even vestigial markings left.

"How on earth could you let it get like this?"

Solange didn't see why not. She began to pull the remains of the net to bits.

"Don't! We may have to make do with that." I was beginning to realise that I wouldn't ever know the Marignys. "Will you ask your mother to get someone to see to it?"

"To see?"

"Clean it up, put it in order." I seized a head of the yellow daisies that were growing all over the place and swung them like a racquet. "Not that I'll put up much of a game in this heat."

"Maman will not permit."

"You mean she won't let us play?"

"She will not think it necessary to clean the tennis." Solange put a finger on one of the posts and rocked it in its socket. "There is no one to do it, everybody is working."

"Then we'll have to do it ourselves. We'll get Valentin to help."

"I do not think it necessary either," said Solange.

I ignored that. I worked on that court, day after day, and got Solange and Valentin to work too whenever I could, which wasn't often. It took days of weeding, raking, making do, mending and marking before we could play.

Solange wasn't keen even then, though I found that she played well enough while she kept her attention on the game. Every so often she would drop her racquet and walk away smiling and shaking her head just as I was about to serve.

"J'en ai assez—tu as l'air si drôle!"

"What do you mean—funny?" I said furiously the first time it happened.

"You are so feroce—" Solange giggled. "Like a man killing a pig."

"There's no such word as 'feroce' in English and you've never seen a man kill a pig."

"I have seen Uncle Dubosque do it."

"I don't look like Uncle Dubosque—how dare you!"

"Dare? Qu'est-ce-que c'est?"

It was not a word she needed, as I was to find out. She was neither bold nor rebellious, she had no principles of her own or anyone else's to rebel against. I wonder what she thought of principles and what people had them for. Mine always amused her.

We took lunch and dinner with Maître and Madame Marigny. At table I heard the family talking together. I marvelled how they talked: not sporadically, turning up subjects as we might stones and dropping them, but bringing out opinions, airing, flashing, fooling with them and never for a moment getting saddled.

Sometimes the subjects were ones on which I considered I was more of an authority than they could ever be—when the conversation turned to London, for instance, or tennis. They heard my solid facts politely, then they were off again at their own pace and I couldn't compete with Madame Marigny chasing, and being chased, by some windy notion; with Maître Marigny, acid and sibilant; with Solange, making an extreme stand for the fun of it; with Valentin, pushing his abstractions, or even with Chelle, just laughing and darting out her tongue. They didn't want information, they wanted entertainment. They didn't want truth, I thought angrily, they wanted to hear themselves.

It was no better if visitors were present. The pace might be faster or they might range farther, depending on the company, but so far as I could see, French people were all the same, they didn't want nor could they give a straight answer.

When the priest came to lunch I knew he was there before I saw or heard anything of him. He had a strong sweetish smell—of Catholic holiness, I supposed. By all accounts Father Benedict was an especially holy man, the Marignys conceded that without argument, they listened with even a touch of deference when he talked, and he talked as much, if not about as much, as they did.

He was youngish, cream-faced, with a lavendar jaw. I stood a little in awe of him, but pleasantly, because he was spruce and kind. That sexless garment, the soutane, and that sort of carnival hat with a pom-pom on top, became him. I liked the look of him and I think he liked the look of himself—which gave a touch of cruelty and wantonness to what happened.

One day at lunch they talked of the years he had spent working in a leper colony. Madame Marigny said something about physical decay and disgust killing pity and I remember he said one got into the habit of looking at without seeing the faces of one's friends. I thought of that afterwards and hoped it was some help to him.

I couldn't make up my mind that I liked Solange. It seemed to hinge on whether I could approve of her, but of course it was the other way about—my principles weren't all that developed. Sometimes I liked her very much: sometimes she let me in, or went where I could follow. Skins were down between us, we had the run of each other and I didn't question anything she did. At other times there was no knowing and I told myself there was nothing I cared to know. Solange always gave me an excuse for an attitude. The day we went to Bordeaux I took up an attitude that was too big for me in the end.

We went on the bus. It was an hour's tedious journey over bad roads with the heat blowing back from the open windows like the blast from an oven. Madame Dubosque knew everybody, she went between the seats talking to each person for the benefit of the whole bus, getting tossed about like a bag of beans. Her hat slipped to the back of her head and she steamed under the armpits, but she talked and clowned in her loud urchin way even, I think, about her new corsets. She tried to bring Solange, who was her favourite, into the fun, but Solange turned her face away.

"I wish she'd shut up," I said irritably. "She makes it hotter."

Solange said that Tin-Tin was making show of herself, to which I agreed and we looked along our noses at the old woman. It didn't stop us from eating the ice-cream and cakes she bought for us in Bordeaux.

Being my first experience of French pastries I ate too many of the richest and rarest. I felt sick, too sick to go to the corsetière with Madame Dubosque. So she took us into a church near the pastry-cook's for safety as well as coolness, and told us to wait for her there.

It was a nice church and I would have been content to sit quietly in the semi-dark, but Solange started pacing about as soon as Madame Dubosque had gone. I said could I help it if I felt sick and she said yes, I'd made a pig of myself. It looked bad, she said, particularly as Tin-Tin had to pay for our refreshments out of her own pocket. I had thought that Madame Marigny was standing treat, but Solange said her mother did not think of that sort of thing, and I could well believe it. When I proposed to reimburse Madame Dubosque, Solange said I'd get my ears boxed if I tried, and that I could believe too.

Solange wouldn't stay in the church. She was going to see the 'momies', she said, and I followed her though I dreaded the heat that was rammed down into the streets.

Close by was a tower. Solange paid some money to the man who sat at the door. I asked her what 'momies' were, but all she would say was that they were 'très historique' and I could write about them in my school essay.

We went down steps into a round stone room. I had only begun to suspect Solange and to be ready for her. After that day I realised that she had means and a mind that were beyond me. She would always go one or two better, and if I couldn't foresee what she would do I should, for my own sake, foresee that she would always do something.

The room was lit, not brightly, by an oil lantern standing on the floor, It was, in fact, only a few degrees less than pitch dark down there, probably with some idea of heightening the

68

effect. A blaze of electricity would have left nothing to the imagination and in this case imagination was more merciful.

The figures were propped round the walls. They were as Solange had said, 'mummies', flesh harder than wood, drier than leather, and about as human as a meteorite. I couldn't reason it out then, but I believe that's what upset me most, that's what made it such a laugh. I don't know who for—not for me, not for anyone who looked at them. There were about thirty and every one was fixed in some horror, or oddity or agony. Some were arched, the head forced back and out of joint, their jaws hung down their necks—they were the idiot dead. A child had the skirt of her dress and a hole where her chest should be; a priest had part of his cassock and his hands out, like claws, in a parody of blessing; a woman carried the cadaver of her baby, sliced like a specimen, in her dried-up womb.

The lantern made liquid shadows, they all seemed to be flowing upwards and never getting away. I looked into their faces, the holes and sockets, the congealed eyeballs, the red and black hair stuck to the bone, and I felt that a nightmare was coming true.

Solange said they had come from a common grave, preserved by the nature of the soil they were buried in eight hundred years ago. She touched them, rapped with her knuckles on their heads and chests and they gave out a solid sound like hide. She picked up a woman's breasts and flapped them, cracked her fingernail against the vitrified child in the womb, without disgust or much interest.

People turn old clothes over like that and thumb second-hand books. I couldn't stand it and I thought then that it was the irreverence of what she was doing to dead people that I couldn't stand. But now I think it was because she couldn't see the laugh, that the laugh was on her, on us all, and I couldn't bear for her not to see it.

I asked her to stop, but of course she wouldn't, not while she thought she was shocking me.

"Voici un sale type," she said, smiling and tapping one of the mummies on its thighs. So I went away up the steps

69

and left her there and as I came out into the heat of the sun it no longer made me feel sick, it made me feel full of juice.

Looking back now, the summer at Bonneval is less like a succession of days than one long day and a sample night.

After dark the Château closed up and withdrew, it became a bubble place holding above miles of woods and plain. The heat of the day relaxed, but only to blood temperature, there was no real sense of release, and moving about under the dim lights indoors or the darkness outside I always felt that we were inside our selves.

The bats flew about at night, very fast and vivid, a pelting of blackness that made it unnerving to walk out of doors. I remember the monstrous beetles that bumbled round the lights and fell, buzzing and dying, into my hair, and I remember that the towers turned pewter colour after dark and the fairy-tale effect was laid on with a trowel, but there was a goblin side too, because by the same process the crimson hangings in my bedroom took on the colour of viscera round about dawn.

I remember footsteps gritting on the terrace and smelling Maître Marigny's brown cigarettes, and when there was a wedding party at a farm miles away I heard the singing and dancing. It was so still I heard it all, down to the clatter of their knives and forks and the scrape of their chairs on the stone.

In that summer in a day events seem to me now to have had a morning or an evening feel. Chelle's battle with the bailiff, for instance, is all noon. We used to hear about it at lunch. Chelle brought her business worries to the family for sympathy and, I suspected, some practical advice. She got neither from Maître Marigny. Solange told me that he refused to have anything to do with his wife's property. He was a lawyer, but so far as he was concerned Bonneval was outside the law. It was well known that anyone might poach and pilfer, cheat and fiddle with impunity. The Maître would not trouble himself this side of Bordeaux and Madame

Marigny was no business woman. That left only Chelle, who was certainly a business child.

Whenever possible what was produced on the estate in the way of wood and fruit—even the sweet chestnuts were harvested by the indefatigable Chelle—provided on a barter system for something that was not produced: for butter, coal, bacon. A man called Pochart looked after the timber. There was a considerable acreage. Pochart had a cottage in the woods and a small cutting-plant and was recognised as a scoundrel. No one thought of sacking him, an honest bailiff was apparently as easy to find as an apple without a core.

Villainy Chelle must expect to cope with if she coped at all. Pochart was also known to have an illicit still in the woods, to manufacture his own spirits and to drink them. Everyone called him 'Pochard', which means 'boozer'— Chelle was also expected to cope with that. Madame Marigny didn't give it a thought anyway, and Maître Marigny had washed his hands of the property and everything pertaining to it, his daughter's safety included. I wondered what my parents would have made of that.

Chelle coped, I believe, as well as anyone could. She lacked years and experience, but she had the power to frighten Pochart out of his wits. When roused she was less than human, and anything to do with money could rouse her. Pochart had been known to swear that she wasn't a child, she was a devil.

Chelle haunted him. She believed he was selling timber behind her back, and all that summer, if she wasn't poring over her ledger in the office, she was in the woods trying to catch Pochart. She crept about like an Indian, Solange said she could move through brushwood without cracking a twig. Sometimes we would be lazing in the shade, not talking, the air still enough to hear the creak of the oxen's harness a mile away as they went round the vines, and we would look up and she'd be beside us, thin as a twig, with her old faded frock shrunk up to her knees and one of Monsieur Dubosque's split straw-hats weighing down on her ears.

I saw her in one of her rages once. It was unnerving, I wouldn't have thought there was room in her for so much passion. We were half-way through lunch when she came in, slipping silently as ever into her chair. Her hands were unwashed and there was sawdust in the roots of her hair. Madame Marigny reprimanded her, she apologised and poured herself a finger of red wine which she diluted with water. Solange asked her what she'd been doing. Chelle said she had been occupied with a serpent, a 'serpente à sonnettes'—a rattlesnake.

"Dans notre forêt?" asked Madame Marigny, taken with the idea, and Chelle said yes, in their forest. Valentin wanted to know if she had killed it and Chelle said she intended to next time she saw it. She took up a knife to show us—first she would dig out its eyes, then she would cut off its hands, then its feet—

"Feet? Hands?" said Valentin. "On a snake?"

"It was Pochard, wasn't it?" said Solange.

Chelle cried out that Pochart was a beast, a drunken pig, she would crush him like a cockroach.

"Tu as un ménagerie, ma petite," said Maître Marigny, relaxing his scars.

Chelle rose to her feet. Her face darkened horribly, it wasn't blood under her skin but some bitter gall. She spoke so fast, spitting out the words, that I couldn't follow the sense. Solange told me afterwards that Chelle had discovered that Pochart was allowing someone to cut wood in the forest and pocketing the money.

Chelle's anger was fantastic. She was consumed with it and it wasn't righteous, it was evil. I couldn't take my eyes off her. The child had become a monster, brilliant with venom. Her bones, arms, hands, even her spine, were hooked out of all humanity, and as she crouched over the table I thought that if Pochart was a cockroach she was a spider.

Maître Marigny went on eating his lunch, so did Valentin. Solange, smiling, crumbled bread. Madame Marigny murmured, "Chérie, chérie—"

Chelle did not hear. She was spitting Pochart's name and out of her mouth it came as an obscenity. I kept wondering what my parents would have thought or what anyone at home would have made of her. She was nine years old and she froze my blood.

Maître Marigny said, without looking up, "Assieds-toi," and Chelle obeyed. She sat down as if a switch had been thrown and a current stopped.

Madame Marigny appealed to her husband. "Qu'est-ce nous allons faire, alors?"

He shrugged. Chelle, a grubby child again, picked the sawdust out of her hair.

"Pochard!" Her tongue flickered out with the name on it.

Valentin's trouble with his father was no doubt a trouble for years, but to me it was all at tea-time because it came to one of its heads then.

Madame Marigny had what she called 'English tea' out of a silver pot, with hot milk and biscottes, at half-past four, on the terrace under the trees. One afternoon a business acquaintance of Maître Marigny's arrived. He was motoring through to Spain and professed great interest in seeing where Edouard Brindille had lived and died. Maître Marigny showed him round and brought him on to the terrace for tea.

I don't think the Maître was pleased to see this man. He was very courteous to him, but towards everyone else he was more than usually acid.

Solange and I had been knocking up on the tennis-court, we were hot and untidy, though I don't think we deserved his comment, as he presented us, about dirt being the privilege of the very young and the very old and only those of the years between must wash. We took our biscottes and sat at a distance on the stone balustrade where Solange amused herself trying to catch lizards.

Valentin had been lying on his back in the shade since lunch, only a yard or so from the tea-table. Maître Marigny ignored him, it was Madame who called him to be presented to the visitor.

Valentin was less presentable than we were. He wore a singlet and dirty shorts, his chest and arms were tripper's

73

pink and peeling from the sun. He got up, blinking. Gravel was stuck all over his bare shoulders and Solange said, "Qu'il est paresseux!" with amusement.

I wasn't sure. If Valentin's questions were so unnecessary that only a lazy person would ask them, on the other hand a lazy person wouldn't seek so diligently for an answer. That afternoon he had told me that he proposed to examine the subject of death because at his age he could look at it academically and he had asked, politely, if I had yet considered the question. I said what question? Everyone died and there was the end of it. Of course Valentin wanted to know if it might not be the beginning or at least the middle of something else.

"You mean Heaven and all that?" I wasn't scornful, I had been brought up to take it for the top end of my scale of values.

But Valentin said death was nothing to do with religion, which startled me because I had always thought that dying was a Biblical thing.

I was sorry for Valentin, being called away from his meditations to face a complete and critical stranger. Watching him shamble over to the tea-table, I wondered if he might even question his father's visitor on the subject of death. I wouldn't have put it past him, he was eager, he seemed to hunger for other people's slants.

Madame Marigny, who had stayed seated only long enough to pour tea for the guest, went behind her son and presented him with a flourish, hands on his head, framing him as if he were a delectable picture. She saw nothing to be ashamed of, she never did see anything in front of her nose, she had to look over her shoulder.

The visitor's name was Latour. He wore a cream flannel suit striped with grey and smoked cigarettes through a silver holder. Solange and I had already entertained him, his smile as we were introduced was entirely to himself. Confronted with Valentin, he looked from him to Maître Marigny and back again with barely concealed surprise.

Of course they were chalk and cheese, or rather jet and cheese, a pop-eyed dreamy boy with his skin in shreds and his bare toes fishing in the dirt, and a senior lawyer dressed for the law in his sombre suit and his pure lawful linen, his burned-out face and his fingers tented together.

Solange said softly, "For papa it is—what do you call 'ennuyer'?"

"Boring?"

"It is boring that this man comes and sees us like this. He is a great talker, he will tell everyone."

Madame Marigny suddenly went off on one of her forays to the far end of the terrace, leaving Valentin facing the two men. Monsieur Latour asked him if he liked games. Valentin said no. Monsieur Latour suggested, with an eye to his grubbiness, that he was perhaps of a mechanical bent. Was it engines that interested him? Valentin shook his head. What then did interest him? Valentin smiled and shrugged. There was an awkward pause, the visitor toyed with his cigarette-holder.

Valentin, ducking his head politely, turned to go, but Maître Marigny, who had so far not said a word, called out sharply, "Attendez!"

Valentin waited. He looked at his father and Maître Marigny looked at him with the corrosive stare he used on his foes and friends alike. There was another pause, it was loaded and as it went on it became quite suffocating. Monsieur Latour said something graceful about the view—he might have been a cicada chirping for all the notice Maître Marigny took.

Solange nudged me. "You are going to see a little comedy."

She might laugh, I didn't think I'd be able to. Valentin pushed his toes into the grit and waited. He wouldn't look up, he was feeling his dirt, I don't think he'd been aware of it until then, no more than an animal is of the dirt on its fur.

Madame Marigny suddenly came hurrying back along the terrace. I thought she'd break things up because she certainly wouldn't notice the atmosphere, but she passed us without a glance and disappeared round the corner of the house.

Maître Marigny looked as if he were preparing a case. It

turned out that he was, against his son. He picked up a spoon and rang it against the side of a cup.

"A quoi est-ce que tu t'intéresses?"

Poor Valentin. No wonder he went a sort of scalded mauve over his sunburn. How could he tell his father what interested him, the 'questions' that he worried at as he mooched and lay about? 'Death,' could he say, "I've been interested in death this afternoon, whether it's a graduation or an end", and trust Maître Marigny to take it as gospel and not as impudence? He did the only thing he could, he shrugged.

Monsieur Latour suggested that it was also the privilege of the young to do nothing. Maître Marigny began interrogating Valentin. It was really a cross-examination conducted, I'm sure, as Maître Marigny would have conducted it in court. Sometimes Valentin got no time to reply, one question was overshot by the next, answered by it, re-formed and presented as a statement of fact that damned or denigrated or poked mild fun with all the wisdom and tolerance on Maître Marigny's side and all the stupidity on Valentin's. Sometimes Valentin was left high and dry, his tongue in his open mouth visibly searching for an answer. Then Maître Marigny would tell him to take time, to think back and not be too modest. One minute he was calling him 'mon fils', 'mon vieux', the next he was firing words, rattling them off the side of the cup with the spoon and laughing—if you could call it laughter, a quacking sound with his mouth going down instead of up.

It was like bringing out a sawmill to cut up a seedling and everybody was embarrassed while it lasted—not for Valentin, for Maître Marigny. He, of all people, was showing off. I'd seen him as a mostly malignant superman who could, if he wished, bring off things that my own father would have blenched at and it was a shock to me to find him out in such a childish failing. Valentin looked sick, even his shame was for his father, not for himself.

Madame Marigny ended the scene. She came running out of the library with Brindille's book and oblivious of anything but her duty as hostess, began to pour tea and read poetry for Monsieur Latour.

Solange got the giggles as Madame Marigny's high murmurous voice took over from her husband's, and the visitor, dazed by the switch, had to ease a finger under his collar. Valentin remained where he was, head bent, until a click of his father's fingers released him.

Shortly after, Chelle raced by in her shrunken dress, shrieking and battering after an escaping hen. Maître Marigny waved a hand at her and told Monsieur Latour that this also was his child. He probably felt that his debasement should be complete.

I expected that that would be the end of it and a good thing too, but next day Solange told me that Valentin was to go to St Cyr.

"A school for soldiers," she said.

"Does he want to be a soldier?"

"Idiot! It is my father who thinks it will be good for him."

"Good?"

"Teach him to march and shoot and stick his neck up."

"But he'll hate it—"

"Of course. Or my father would not do it."

"But why?"

"To pay him. My father always pays people."

That I could believe. "But Valentin isn't people, he's his son."

"You are a fool, Rose."

I sought out Valentin. "Is it true you have to go to military school?"

"My father has said so."

"That's awful! You won't like it at all!"

"Don't disturb yourself," Valentin said kindly. "I shall not be a soldier."

I didn't see how he could get out of it and I was relieved when Madame Marigny asked the Curé to speak to her husband.

Solange, Valentin and I were setting off for a walk one afternoon and we met Father Benedict on his way up to the Château.

He greeted us gaily. "I am glad to have seen you, Valentin, because I am about to talk to your father on the subject of your—" he winked—"military training."

Valentin murmured something about its not being necessary.

"Then you wish to go to St Cyr?"

"I do not," said Valentin definitely.

"Perhaps you think I have no influence with Monsieur le Maître?"

"It isn't that. I beg your pardon, Father, I'm very grateful to you for taking the trouble."

"Ah well," said the Curé briskly, "we shall soon see what is necessary."

"I'm glad you're going to try, anyway," I said in English. "It's awful to think of Valentin stabbing sandbags and all that."

The Curé raised his eyebrows, but when Solange had translated he burst out laughing. "My child," he said kindly, 'ma petite' I think he called me, which sounds much nicer— "St Cyr is not like that, never fear. It is a complete education, a very fine one." He turned to Valentin. "What do you wish to do?"

"Do?"

"In life you will wish to do something, to be something."

"I don't wish to be," Valentin said calmly. 'I *am*."

"That is enough?"

Solange laughed. "It is enough that he is lazy."

The Curé shook his head. "Valentin is not lazy. When his mind enquires he cannot choose but try to answer it."

He smelt holy even in the sunshine. It was a pity his faith was misdirected: being Roman Catholic was not as bad as being an unbeliever, but I did wonder what the position was with regard to godliness that did not come from the right God.

He was saying to Valentin, without irony or fun, "How have you answered?"

"I haven't, but I will."

"You believe there is an answer to everything?"

"Of course." Valentin added cryptically, "We are complete."

"Only in God," said the Curé.

It occurred to me that his God could be the right one approached through the wrong channels. It occurred to me also that I knew little about Roman Catholicism. What did they believe? Something to do with the Virgin Mary. I supposed God wouldn't be too hard on them for worshipping his own mother.

"Is it wrong to ask?" said Valentin.

"A question is not wrong. The answer may be."

"Sans doute," Solange said unkindly, "when he takes his bachot."

"Do you always ask yourself, my son?" said the Curé. "Do you never ask God?"

"I've been given a brain and I intend to use it." Valentin said roughly, "I don't expect God to tell me everything. Do you?"

"I have no other expectations."

There was a special intimacy in his voice, at once humble and proud. We all felt a bit put out and wouldn't look at him, though he was looking at us and out of the corner of my eye I saw that he was bringing us into his smile.

He left us to go on to the Château. We watched him stride away, ornate and black, his cassock swinging gracefully. At the bend of the path he turned to wave.

"Perhaps he is stupid," said Valentin.

"He's good," said Solange. "That makes him very happy."

I said to Valentin, "It's jolly nice of him to go and talk to your father. If anyone can make him change his mind, the Curé will."

"My father won't send me to St Cyr."

"How do you know?" He shrugged, but I insisted. "Why won't he?" and I remember that Valentin, who was polite and always talked to me in English, lapsed into French.

"Il s'en fiche."

"What?"

"He doesn't care enough to do it." He went to where the

79

dust was thickest and hottest and pushed his bare feet into it, one at a time. "I would prefer if he did."

Solange said scornfully, "You would prefer he should take you up like his little dog and keep you in his lap. You would prefer he should not let you out of his sight so there should be nothing for you to do, nowhere for you to go."

Valentin went on slowly and pleasurably running the hot dust into his toes.

"Well that is not what I want," said Solange. "No one shall tell me what to do. I shall do always as I wish." She had her hands on her hips, teasing us. "I wish already there was no papa, no maman, no Valentin, no Chelle, no Rose to tell me what to do—"

"I don't tell you what to do!"

She picked up my plait of hair and danced round me with it as if I were a maypole. "You tell me, but I don't do it."

I expect I did try to tell her. It was inconceivable to me how everything slipped away in that household. At home when we talked we planned, even if it was just how to remake the garden, or a day's outing, and we carried through our plans. The Marignys talked of 'l'année dernière', but never of the future and not of the present with any decision. Chelle was the only one who did anything. They really were 'en vacance' at Bonneval: if not content with, they were acquiescent in its timelessness. At home every day had its character whether it was a holiday or not. I could have been dropped out of the blue into Beckenham and I'd have known at once that it was Monday or Friday. And imagine not being able to tell Sunday!

At Bonneval there was no use for the days of the week or the time of the day. You could walk through the village and it would be shuttered against the heat, there might be a chicken scratching about and an old woman emptying a pail—there was always an old woman doing something. They opened the shutters and sat outside their houses and played boules in the road when it got a little cooler, which was when the sun went down, which was as near as they came to clock time. I suppose they had no business with it, only needs—theirs and the land they worked. They got hungry so they had a meal, they got tired so they went to bed: the seasons came round, they might be soon or they might be late, but that had nothing to do with the calendar. On Sundays everyone went to Mass, I daresay only because the church bell reminded them.

The weather did have something to do with it. In a colder or a wetter climate they'd have hustled about. Here, where the same prodigal heat was spent on the green grapes and the dust in the ditches there was no incentive, the air would have blunted anything like a qualm or a worry.

The Marignys probably gave themselves up to it the moment they got off the train. I used to wonder what they were like in Paris. I couldn't imagine them anywhere but here, what they were here I took to be their basic selves, stripped of business and social etceteras.

But perhaps they weren't complete and that would explain why they seemed to be lacking, why they didn't take anything seriously—because they didn't take Bonneval seriously.

I didn't think of it then, to me they were irresponsible people, especially Maître Marigny who held himself in abeyance. Still wearing his dark formal clothes he appeared at intervals for meals or a constitutional on the terrace. He was so acid and dry that even the heat couldn't involve him. I don't remember ever seeing him put out a hand to anyone, and when he interrogated Valentin in front of Monseiur Latour he used a probe, not his finger.

Solange said it was because he disliked Bonneval. He went there on sufferance, not by so much as one word of advice would he help his wife manage her property. He wanted it ruined or shut up, most of all he wanted it sold.

"Then we could have a villa at Arcachon," said Solange. "A cake house, you know?"

"A what?"

She squared her hands. "Like this, very à la mode, and white like an iced cake. We would have a roof garden and sun umbrellas and you, my poor Rose, would swim all day in the sea and make your chests big."

"Chest," I told her sharply. "It's singular unless you're talking about several people. And I'm not keen on swimming."

Actually I was with Maître Marigny about the villa, it would be more fun than Bonneval. I also felt that Madame Marigny was right to keep the Château in the family.

Even in those days when everything was cheaper it must have cost a lot to maintain. She tried to make it self-supporting, but she was no manager and there was only Chelle to watch her interests.

Chelle cared, Chelle was serious, Chelle had made herself responsible and that was the last straw, the final affront to common sense and normality. A nine-year-old child running a business, juggling with the accounts, haggling, cheating and being cheated, her father not bothering to look on and her mother not knowing what she was looking on. If I told them that at home they wouldn't believe me, they'd think it was only how it seemed.

One day we took a barrowload of small plums—'mirabelles', they were called—to one of the farms to be exchanged for butter. We were all going because the barrow was heavy and Chelle couldn't manage it by herself. At the last moment Madame Marigny said she would come too. Chelle pulled a face. Solange told me that Chelle liked everything on a business footing whereas her mother was apt to play the 'grande dame'.

We set off, Valentin and Chelle trundling the barrow, Solange and I on either side to keep the plums from toppling, and Madame Marigny strolling in the rear. It was a long walk to the farm. We had to wait while Madame Marigny made sorties to pick wild flowers and examine the butterflies and other insects. We were more like four adults and she the child. She kept exclaiming and running after us with this and that and once we lost sight of her completely. The only clue was some gigantic yellow cow parsley threshing about as she moved among it.

"Quelle idiote!" raged Chelle.

When we drew near the farm two huge, gaunt dogs rushed at us, barking savagely. Chelle screamed at them and they slunk round behind us, growling. Madame Marigny, harassed by the dogs, dropped her flowers. I was going back to pick them up for her but Solange said, "Leave them, they are rubbish," and called sharply, "Dépêche-toi, maman!"

I was sorry for Madame Marigny, but I need not have been. She hadn't noticed that her flowers were gone. As we reached the house two women ran out, one hastily pinning up her hair and the other pulling at her apron. Madame Marigny greeted them serenely and they chased the chickens out of her path and ushered her in with as much bowing and hand spreading as if it were a golden coach instead of a broken-down farmhouse.

Chelle shovelled some plums into the skirt of her dress and went off with it held up above her skinny thighs.

Solange said, "Maman is a fool, Chelle is a peasant."

Valentin took my arm. "Come, Rose, you shall see this farm."

It was a surprising place. First we looked into the room where Madame Marigny was being entertained. The women had brought out a bottle of wine and Madame Marigny was sitting at one end of a huge settle. The other end was piled with blankets and a quilt as if it were used for a bed. The room was very big but crowded, besides the furniture there were barrels and baskets and logs and sacks and half-plucked chickens and more blankets heaped on the floor.

"They cannot sleep upstairs," said Valentin. "The roof is fallen."

The ceiling of this room didn't look very safe. It was cracked from end to end, black with smoke and cobwebs and hung with skeleton bunches of herbs, sides of bacon and the bodies of hares with bloody bags over their noses.

Madame Marigny sipped her wine. The women were talking to her both at once, pouring out troubles long bottled up or glorying in something—I couldn't tell which. They had urchin voices and a strange accent.

Valentin said they were Normans. They worked well but were bad-tempered.

I said they weren't very clean either and he smiled. "You will see."

I certainly had a surprise when I saw the animals' quarters. They were a miracle of cleanliness and modernity, tiled in white and equipped with running water and electric light. The stove where the pig-swill was cooking would have put many a kitchen range to shame for the depth of its polish. I think the pigs themselves had been scrubbed, their trotters were like newly shone shoes.

One of the sons was a hunchback. He wore a torn singlet, the lump on his spine stretching it taut like a fist in a glove. He followed us round, bursting with pride and talking incomprehensible Norman French. We had to see everything, the cows—curry-combed and immaculate; the young bull with a hide like velvet and a gold ring through his nose; the horses, bright as chestnuts, their manes and tails hanging smoother than my own hair. One slender mare with a wild white eye was kept to pull the black-and-silver gig: the man fetched an egg and cracked it for her and she ate it and delicately dropped the shell into his hand.

"You see, Rose," said Valentin, "the beasts live like people and the people live like beasts." The hunchback nodded and grinned at us, showing his black teeth.

Chelle came back to the barrow of plums followed by the farmer. He was saturnine and unshaven, black beard guttered down his jaw, he had the pink-rimmed angry eyes of a pig. But Chelle looked a match for him, she was sharpened up for business, talking as fast, and to me as incomprehensibly, as the hunchback.

She was picking up plums and displaying them in her palm, she broke one open and thrust it at the farmer, thrust it right into his mouth. He spat it out immediately. Thereupon Chelle worked her arms in deep and brought up plums from the bottom of the barrow to prove that they were as good as the top ones. This man was not talkative, he walked round the barrow, estimating its capacity, and then he said something which caused Chelle to throw up her hands and try to wheel the barrow away. She couldn't, the load was too heavy. Shoving, scarlet in the face, she shouted over her shoulder. Whatever it was seemed to anger the farmer. He spat in her direction, kicked at a chicken that came near his boot and went into the house. Chelle followed him, so did Valentin and I, as far as the doorway.

I found it embarrassing, this palaver to get a pound or two of butter on the cheap. Madame Marigny had money to buy it at the shop, she did anyway when there were no mirabelles. I would have preferred to do without butter altogether than tangle with these people.

Madame Marigny wasn't tangling. She was in the farm-house kitchen sipping wine and the two women were with her. They were still talking, with battering tongues and hedgerow-gipsy faces turning and swooping. The farmer was in the doorway and the hunchback had come in from the yard. Solange leaned against the wall. Everyone was there, everyone standing except Madame Marigny, who sat smiling through a cloud of grace.

The younger woman suddenly crouched down and pulled her dress off her shoulders and showed her back covered with liver-blue bruises. Madame Marigny looked serenely— they might have been marks on the floor—the other woman threw out a spitting of words. Then the farmer said something and whatever it was got through Madame Marigny's cloud. She went pink, china pink spread from her cheeks down to her neck and up under her hair. The hunchback burst out laughing; his jaws working with joy set the women laughing too.

I asked Valentin what it was about and he said that the men beat their wives and the wives liked it. I was hurt, there was no need for a snub, if he didn't want to answer he only had to say so.

The farmer grinned across the room to Madame Marigny. She smiled, tightly at first, then she put up her hand and covered her mouth—she was laughing. Everyone was, except Chelle, gnawing at a plum. The woman with the bruises spun round and round like a top, slapping laughter out of herself.

*

85

I badly wanted the Marignys to commit themselves. If I could have found them out in one thing which they had to stand by, couldn't drift away from, leave high and dry—or low and dirty as they had left the people at the farm—I could have excused them and been comfortable. A proselytising itch wouldn't let me be. I wasn't a crusader, it was just that I had no doubts, I could have put the world right—I didn't need to, of course, because there had never been much wrong with it. That there could be attitudes to life hadn't dawned on me, there was life and there were rules which the Marignys, allowing for foreignness, heat and Catholicism, ought to have kept as everyone else did, except lunatics and criminals. I was lucky I could still believe that at twelve years old: the Marignys, had I known it, were a first gentle intimation that I shouldn't.

All that summer I tried to see where they were pinned down and Solange I tried to pin down where I thought she ought to be. My interrogations of her had a way of coming back to myself. It was difficult to get a straight or satisfactory answer out of her and she invariably turned the tables and heckled me. I entertained rather than puzzled her. She wasn't involved enough to more than wonder, momentarily, about anyone, and I expect she found me a bit of a freak. My interests were games and film stars, and I was a voracious reader of schoolgirl fiction. My world was in Beckenham with outer planets such as Bexhill and Dymchurch where we went for holidays. As soon as I left it Bonneval became a planet too, a lunar and, my tastes being what they were, not such an attractive one.

Solange was a great gossip. She gossiped at me rather than with me. I suspect she was also a fancifier, mystification being her amusement that summer. She wouldn't accept my small talk in kindred spirit, she picked it up for puncturing and twisting and open scorn. I had to take some sweeping if not crashing statements from her, and if I jibbed she would either be French and shrug, or Marigny and bubble.

When I knew that she and Chelle went to a convent school in Paris I imagined them learning only sewing and enough Latin to read their missals. I was surprised, and chagrined, to find that Solange took the same subjects as I did and her class at school was farther advanced in all of them. By her account that was, and she wasn't likely to dream up American history which we hadn't begun, and trigonometry which was still a threat. On the other hand, did nuns know about such things? Weren't they limited to holy ritual, lives of the saints and Hail Mary's?

It was the sort of discrepancy I encountered with all the Marignys: there was Chelle, touting plums and haggling over a pound of butter they could well afford to buy: Valentin, asking himself questions that weren't intended for answering: Maître Marigny, a legal eminence letting his wife be rooked by peasants; and Bonneval, which was historic because of Brindille and slightly comic because of the hatpin and which none of them wanted. Even Chelle who fought to keep it wanted the fight, not Bonneval.

I thought I had a logical sticking point in Solange's attitude to religion and I could have been satisfied with just that. After all, she was a foreigner, her religion was not right nor proper nor even clean—witness, thought I, their saints and martyrs, the awful and dirty lengths they went to get sanctified—but better for Solange to believe even that sort of thing because I could at least relinquish her. If she believed nothing at all I couldn't see how to accept her in the first place.

We talked about Catholicism. I asked and she answered and on the whole she was ready to answer, she was explicit. She must have been irritated by my crassitude, and she had reason. I shudder now to think of the things I said: why did Catholics worship the mother of God instead of God Himself? Did their priests wear skirts because their God was a woman? Was it true that they could sin all day provided they confessed in the evening? Or that they could pray first and sin after—the bigger the sin the longer the prayer, and for robbery to murder they could pray on the instalment system? Did Solange think she was married to Christ? What did she actually say as she told her beads?

Solange, who was ready enough in other respects to mock and mystify, showed herself patient and sincere when it came to answering my stupid questions about her faith. She really seemed to want to make me understand, ignorance such as mine was an offence.

"We cannot lose our sin unless we resolve also to be better. And this we must do from the heart. Nous devons promettre de tout coeur de ne jamais commetre ces mêmes péchés."

"Anyone can promise anything, and mean it at the time. If you eat too much chocolate you can promise never to touch it again and that's not being saved, that's being sick."

"I think anyway it is the same thing for the stomach and for the heart."

I wasn't interested in the Catholic faith so much as in Solange's. I got the impression that neither could be lightly put aside. I was a bit disappointed to find that Catholicism wasn't so lurid and fetishtistic as I'd thought, and this brought Solange a peg or two nearer my estimation of normal.

I was easier with her while I could believe in her belief, and I was ready to take the rest of the family on the same terms, which shows how hard put I was to find others. Though I wasn't devout, I could no more visualise the Establishment without a Heaven than a room without a ceiling. God went without saying, so did the fact that one cleaned one's teeth before going to bed. It was on fundamentals rather than terms that I was taking the Marignys and stretching the point because to my mind their fundamentals were sadly misplaced. For the first time since coming to Bonneval I was, if not reassured, at least resigned to these people. I could let them alone. Latched on to heresy, I could feel pity for their delusion.

It was Solange's idea to go to a confirmation service in the local church. She may have meant it to enlighten me but more likely she hoped it would be entertaining for us all.

There weren't many occasions made for us at the Château. As I've said, we were left to our own devices. For one reason and another Solange never did come to stay with me, but if she had, my parents would have taken us about and shown her everything of interest and I dare say we'd even have hankered after some time to ourselves.

Anything we did that was rounded and eventful, like the visit to Bordeaux, as distinct from the long blanket-day at the Château, has a place in my mind like furniture in a room, and what happened in the church at Bonneval is furniture that I cannot shift or do away with.

Details persist, irrelevancies have combined over the years to give the event its special inhumanity and horror. I remember Solange's dress, which was bright yellow, the colour of cheap lemonade and I thought wrong for going to church in. And my hat, a white straw trimmed with cornflowers, had simply been my best until then. Thereafter it acquired a significance, a dedication to the day. Solange twisted a chiffon scarf round her hair and looked ten years older. She probably wanted to, it was only a little while since she had been confirmed, but I was very conscious of her seeming sophistication.

Valentin came to the service though he chose not to walk with us. He followed about a hundred yards behind and when we stopped he stopped too and stood with his head down like a waiting horse. Solange said he was 'affairé' and when I said that he didn't look busy she said that I didn't look anything although I was, she supposed, some classifiable lump of something.

It was uncalled-for, I wasn't criticising Valentin, but she would have said it anyway, out of the blue if necessary. I think she had been waiting to deliver it as a pronouncement rather than a gibe because it was her concluded and irrevocable opinion of me.

I wasn't used to being misjudged. People tended to trust me and take my word on the very face value that Solange denied. That she, slippery and equivocal, should be the one to deny it proved her own insufficiency. So I managed to think, and was ready to tell her, but I didn't get the chance. The bell rang for the service and she started to run and Valentin came up and put his fists in our backs, hustling us. I remember the dirt smoking up as we ran and it seemed to me to epitomise the moral and spiritual poverties of the place. This Catholic place. What else could I blame, apart from its not being English?

That smell which the Curé had about him, of hot pencils and wax, was a power inside the small church. To me it was like a great aromatic sleeve that would wrap round and stifle those who clung to it. It is, now, the sweet holy smell of what happened.

There were six children being confirmed, three girls and three boys. Confirmed in what? They came, two by two, down the aisle, the girls in white dresses and veils like brides and the boys in their best suits with white sashes on their left arms. Each carried a small wreath of white flowers. I looked at them with curiosity as if they were going to damnation: to my way of thinking, they were.

The church was filled with women in black and some younger children wearing clean pinafores. They had dressed up, put on something special and the Curé was there with a sort of embroidered bookmarker round his neck, all bloomy in the light of the candles. That's the colour of it, that pinky gold, tender and grand—I've hated it ever since.

There was an enormous figure of St Thérèse of Lisieux haloed with roses. Behind every rose blazed an electric light bulb. It all looked as if the paint was still wet, the Saint's apple cheeks and yellow sausage curls glistened with newness. I thought of our chemist's shop at home where they had something very similar, except for the roses—an eight-foot model of Hygeia to advertise health salts.

I sat down, I was present as an observer and had no intention of taking part in the service. Someone would see that, I thought, and nudge someone else and that would go on until they all knew that there was an unbeliever in their midst and then they would murmur and the murmur would grow to a clamour, drowning the singing and the organ music and they would turn on me and buffet me with their hands and throw me out because I wasn't one of them. It didn't frighten me, I folded my arms across my chest and frowned at the altar. I felt absolutely right, a bulwark of truth in the midst of heresy.

No one took any notice of me, except Father Benedict

who smiled and lifted his hand, almost waving, over the heads of the children. They sang, standing shoulder to shoulder. Everybody sang, the organist loudest of all. She was a young, fat woman in a fruit hat and she had the lungs of a London coster. I didn't sing though I'd have liked to, it was as rousing, whatever they were singing, as 'We plough the fields and scatter', which is my favourite hymn. I looked up at the roof to show disapproval and disassociation, then I worried lest they might think I was praying. I couldn't look down at the floor for the same reason, so I stared in front of me at a swarthy boy in a frilled shirt and long white socks. He is the only one of the children I remember individually and his the only reactions. The rest massed together like the general hubbub of a storm.

The children being confirmed had to walk in procession round the church and they formed up, two by two, with robed boys carrying a golden cross and censer in front and the priest following behind them. But they had gone only a few steps when the boy with the frilled shirt ducked out of line and ran back to the congregation. He had forgotten his wreath of flowers—nor could he find it at once because it had dropped under his chair.

The procession came to a bewildered stop, the boys and girls looking back over their shoulders and the last pair, trying to keep going, blundered into the ones in front. Father Benedict was taken aback, he stood with brows raised and hands on his hips, and the organist, craning to see what was happening, played a jumble of wrong chords. Solange, of course, was laughing, and just as the swarthy boy groped under his chair she nudged the wreath out of his reach with her foot.

But he found it. He said, "Le voilà!" and showed it to everyone before he carried it back to his place in the procession hanging from his hand like a spare tyre. The procession shuffled on again with the organ music battering after. Father Benedict followed. He held his hands palm to palm and smiled up as he walked, sharing the joke, I expect, with the angels.

Finally they lined up before the altar and were pledged

to renounce their sins and accept God all their days. By God, of course, I reminded myself, they meant the Virgin. They simply weren't looking high enough, their concepts must be profane or mean if they couldn't grasp the facts of sublime Genesis. Or were they all being kept in the dark for some creaming-off purpose, to afford special privilege and entitlement to the chosen? I found it hard to believe that Father Benedict, for instance, had a mean or profane mind.

I had to admit that wherever his prayers were going they went well. He had a nice tenor voice, every prayer was an aria and I liked the way he used his hands to offer, shape and present what he said. It was so courteous, a change from the apocryphal delivery of our vicar at home; his was a take-it-or-leave-it attitude, even to God.

Listening to Father Benedict I wondered if, after all, the thing, the important thing, might be to pray, the act of faith, to ask of and confide in an almightiness, whatever the name, provided it was an almighty goodness.

This thought, which had never occurred to me before, seemed at once blasphemous and sound. I didn't know what to do with it, but as I sat there it began to settle into a conviction. Perhaps I'd got an answer—though I wasn't the one who made a purpose of asking. The nature of goodness would have seemed to me academic if ever I'd thought about it. Now that I came to think, I saw that it needn't be national or sectarian. It could be, it ought to be, universal. So there wouldn't be quibbles from above at the purely regional labels that were put on it at this end.

It might have been a nice idea to have had at twelve years old if I could have held on to it. I still remember what a spacious feeling it was and I realised even then that there would be more to it than the immediate relief of not being in the company of souls already lost. I was happy, selflessly and spiritually happy for two or three minutes.

Most people have had experiences like that, once or twice in their lifetimes. I read somewhere that such sensations are quite physical in origin, something like the feeling of well-being you can have when you're about to catch a cold, a sort of screwing and priming of all the natural defences of the body. Anyway, it didn't last, I might have become a crank or a missionary if it had.

The Curé had blessed the children and was turned away, praying for them and, I think, for all of us, when the thing happened. There was first a soft stirring sound like a small creature moving about overhead. I looked up but I couldn't see anything.

Father Benedict went on praying. When he stopped it was too late. The rustling was followed by a sharp cracking like a burst of fireworks, then a dragging, tearing noise, and then silence, which was like nothing and kept on and on for days.

It was the figure, the eight-foot-high figure of St Thérèse of Lisieux which had been dedicated only a few months ago and now was breaking from its supports. I have as perfect a picture of that pink vacuous face descending—roses, wiring, plaster-dust and all—as if it had happened in the slowest of slow motion. It seems to me now that there was ample time, there must have been, for Father Benedict to get clear. Someone shouted to him, but he didn't move. He stood there, stopped in his prayer, hands clasped, looking up. He could have saved himself, there was no question of saving anyone else, the children and all of us in the front rows of the congregation had crowded back into the aisles.

Perhaps he was still miles away in his prayer, or perhaps he was paralysed with fright, or it was like a nightmare and he couldn't move. Perhaps he was stupid, as Valentin had said. Anyway, he just waited, not lifting a finger to shield his face, for St Thérèse to hit him.

The statue was of wood and heavy, though I don't think the body of it touched him. The damage was done by an electric light bulb in the halo. The plaster roses came down sideways, with the most momentum, and the bulb, already broken, sheared into his upturned cheek. Then the statue, crashing to the floor, seemed to rebound and twist until it lay with its sausage curls on the altar steps and its big dimpled feet on the altar-cloth. Father Benedict spun round, showing us the terrible havoc of his face, then sank submissively to his knees. There he stayed until the organist ran to

93

him and touched his shoulder. He keeled over then. He had fainted.

As I said, I don't remember anyone's reactions in detail, except the swarthy boy's. There was a lot of noise, screaming women, crying children, someone hysterical, but the silence was where they could not break it. They all crowded round the high altar, it was impossible to see the Curé and I was glad. I stayed where I was, so did the swarthy boy. He sat down and pulled his white wreath to pieces.

After a while Valentin came and took my arm. He said they had sent for the doctor, there was nothing we could do and we had better go.

I was still raw with shock when supper-time came that evening. I'd been close enough to see clearly what the electric light bulb had done to Father Benedict's face. There was something else that was going to worry me if I looked at it, another answer, a likely one, to my question. I was trying not to look at that, but the Marignys picked it up and brandished it at me.

Maître Marigny was thinking of the legal side. He talked about something called the Curia, and compensation from the ecclesiastical furnishers at Angoulême who had made and erected the St Thérèse. I don't know if he was talking seriously or frivolously or to himself. I never could tell with him but I didn't expect him to be human.

I see now that he was the only one who looked at the matter from Father Benedict's standpoint. Perhaps it wasn't Father Benedict's only standpoint, perhaps not the right or final one—I hope it wasn't—but either from kindness or force of professional habit Maître Marigny did give thought to a problem that was not his own.

Madame Dubosque, when she carried in the soup, said that the Father had been taken to hospital in Bordeaux. The local doctor's opinion was that he would lose the sight of one eye and be badly disfigured on the left side of his face. Madame Dubosque blamed the statue itself. It was damned. She had it on good authority—did not her belle-soeur have a cousin in Angoulême?—that it was modelled after the likeness of a local woman of bad repute.

I doubted the likeness, not the reputation—that statue had a face as blank as a button mould.

Solange and Valentin were amused about the model. They teased Madame Dubosque with a knowingness that puzzled and discomforted me. I neither knew what was making them laugh or how they were able to.

Maître Marigny grimaced because the soup was too salty. Madame was lost to some prospect of her own. I didn't have anything to occupy my hands because I wasn't hungry. I stared in front of me until old Tin-Tin leaned across the table and pulled faces at me.

When she had gone to fetch the next course Solange said that perhaps it was fortunate that Monsieur le Curé had had experience among the lepers. I remember how she spoke, politely and formally as she might start a conversation with strangers and I looked for a loophole, a word I had missed. I thought not even Solange would say that, and then Maître Marigny remarked that of course one could see one's own mutilation in every unmarked face.

I looked at Valentin. Had he no questions? Or wasn't this useless enough to ask? I thought, of course not, because it is answerable and they all have the answer. They didn't know that I needed to be told. I should have to make them know. At the risk of ridicule, and of Maître Marigny's sarcasm I must make them see that I badly needed to be told. I had one question to put, it had already made a hundred others, but they could give me their one almighty reason to satisfy the lot.

Maître Marigny began to serve our plates from the main dishes. I always watched him do that, he had such a delicate derogatory method of dissecting the food. He said—and the euphemism bothered me afterwards—that it might be a little difficult for Father Benedict to continue with his chosen career.

"He'll have the other eye," said Solange.

Maître Marigny spoke directly to his wife—something he seldom did—first tapping on her glass to bring her back from wherever she was. Monsieur le Curé, he said, was a vain man in that he had a private mind and a closed religion. He was therefore ambitious, said Maître Marigny, believing that his capacity for good should be given preference. Bonneval was but a phase, he had a goal set. Maître Marigny suspected, wryly, that it entailed a cardinal's hat.

Madame Marigny was attending. She fanned herself with the scarf bit of her dress, she was hot, perhaps, because she was angry.

Her husband went on, as he rolled little round roast potatoes on to our plates, that if Father Benedict's appearance was greatly spoiled he might find himself unacceptable in the sphere of his choice. A lawyer could be disfigured without prejudice to his professional chances—here Maître Marigny tightened his own seamed cheeks—and a priest of character might overcome it. But not Father Benedict.

He meant, I suppose, that what other people saw in him had been Father Benedict's best chance. He may have been right, I hardly knew the Curé, but I thought I knew enough of Maître Marigny to see that he would twist the best of everyone.

Madame Marigny cried, "How ridiculous!" and we waited for her to go on from there. She looked at everyone, except her husband, with her normally protuberant eyes straining out of their sockets, but she spoke not another word.

Solange said, "I shan't mind looking at him."

"Will you mind, Maman?" asked Valentin.

"Of course not."

"When he blesses you?"

"Why should I?"

"When he says Mass will you look at him?"

"Naturally!"

"Won't that be like offering the Host on a broken Paten?" said Solange.

They were teasing her as I would never presume to tease either of my parents, but what sickened me was their teasing on *this* point. I blamed their father for starting it, for acidifying their minds.

I asked my question, I asked why it had happened. I

couldn't see why, I couldn't really, unless I'd been right in the first place and God was a strict God and jealous, and Hell was every other denomination. If that was the case I'd have to ask what was there to choose between earth and a heaven governed with that blend of spite and officialdom. "Why did it happen?" I asked Maître Marigny, but I looked round at them all, I was ready to take the answer from anyone.

"Because the rivets pulled out of the wall," said Valentin.

"Because St Thérèse didn't like the statue," said Solange.

I meant why had it happened to Father Benedict, I said, while he was in church and while he was praying. Solange pretended to take my hand to coax my wits. Where was the statue? The statue was in the church above the altar. And where did the priest most often pray? He prayed at the altar. So where else could it happen?

That was how it happened, I said, but I wanted to know *why*.

For once nobody spoke. Maître Marigny laid down his fork and they all looked at me. I was determined. They knew the reason why, they only had to open a mouth to tell me. I was worried, though, that if Maître Marigny opened his mouth a flow of words would come out which I might not understand. It would be best if Madame answered.

I asked her: "Why did it happen to the Curé, he's a good man, isn't he? And he was praying!"

Although she was looking, it wasn't where one usually does look at other people, but right through my forehead to a spot at the back of my skull. I don't believe she ever looked at anyone, I don't think she would have recognised me if we'd met in the street a week after I left Bonneval.

It was Maître Marigny who answered and he merely said, "God knows."

"But don't you?"

"There would be no need for God if I did." And I remember his pouring and drinking a glass of wine with a briskness that made it plain that he thought me a fool.

Solange often told me that I was 'simpliste'. I was indeed over-simple for my age, but by the time I left Bonneval I began to appreciate that rich and poor, good and bad were only subdivisions because there was, primarily, another sort.

PART THREE

"You must do as you wish."

"I hoped you'd see my reason."

"Believe me, I do."

There was satisfaction in seeing it so clearly, a relief in being able to despise someone so completely. But Rose was angry, too, with an anger which she drew upon. No one had inspired it, not even Cade. The offence was rooted and pertained to the whole business of Hilda Loeb's bequest. Perhaps to more. Rose only knew that she had a fund of rage for moments such as this.

"I was at fault in the first place. If I'd thought twice before agreeing to serve on the Committee I'd have seen how liable I must be to the fear of appropriation—my own fear, of course. It won't help me to do justice either way. Falling over backwards to be fair," said Cade wryly.

"In the very first place I was at fault for asking you. Or should we go back to the place before that and blame Hilda for leaving the money?"

"We were friends, Rose—a good deed can't spoil that."

"One wouldn't think so, but there's the naughty world to complicate matters."

Cade got up with a helpless dusting of his hands and went to the window. He stood looking at his 'sublime' view of potting-shed, clothes-post, currant bushes. He was an ordinary man and it had recommended him to Rose in the past, she had sympathised with his efforts to make himself extraordinary, a man of God. He would never be that, not in a thousand years. It was not that he didn't amount, he wasn't even in the same column as, for instance, Father Benedict.

If any man had the right to assign himself to God, Father Benedict had. He was chosen, marked down, one might say. Apart from his personal disaster and what he had made of it there was a quality about him which she only remembered because it had grown up, later. In conclusion, she might say, and for good and all, he had singularity—which was the first essential for a leader, especially of souls, whereas Eric Cade was not one but a personification of the many.

"If you're not going to serve on the Committee who will look out for the church's needs?"

Cade turned, straight-faced. "I'm sure I can rely on you to do that."

"Can you? I'm not an officer of the church, not even a deaconness. But I'll do my temporal best."

"It's a wonderful thing to know where one's duty is."

He spoke without irony or malice. Rose could detect a hint of wistfulness. She said, "I find no difficulty in this instance."

Cade had nothing to say to that. He relapsed into his thoughts, unhappy ones, which did not appear to include Rose or his present whereabouts.

"Will you stay to tea?"

Previously she would have brought it for them both without asking. Rousing himself, he recognised the distinction.

"Thank you, better not." But he made no move to go.

Rose picked up and folded a newspaper. "Everyone's most concerned about Mrs Peachey, but, relatively speaking, she's comfortable."

"Comfortable?" He, anyway, couldn't have looked bleaker. "Relative to what?"

Rose smoothed the newspaper. "A thousand dead and five thousand homeless in Indo-China. I suppose some of them might envy her."

"She doesn't want much to make her happy."

"That's enviable if through no fault of your own you're left wanting pretty nearly everything."

"Can we refuse her on the grounds that there are others, too many others, we can't help?"

"Of course there are others," Rose said irritably, "there always will be. It's a matter of perspective."

"How you look at it," he said obediently and drifted towards the door. It was valedictory, the way he paused as if to peel off the room. "How do you look at it, Rose?"

"With pity. I do believe, though, that such things are allowed for."

"A pattern?"

He was giving her half his attention, the rest was for the room which he now looked at, round her, so that she was piqued into saying, "Whether it's an earthquake or a rush of blood to the head, violence has to go somewhere that can take it. They don't explode rockets, do they, without fortifying the ground under them?"

He was not sure, she could see, what he had heard, let alone what she meant. She said, sharply, "People are equipped for it—the people that suffer it."

"Equipped? Old people—children?"

"How much do they feel? Actually feel? As much as some of us thinking—*trying* to think—of it? I often try, often enough to know I'm not cut out for the real thing. I shouldn't last," said Rose, "longer than a snowball on a hot griddle."

"So you expect not to suffer the real thing?"

"I trust not to be called upon to."

"I shall pray to God you're not." He opened the door and, turning back, tapped at his pockets. "But He may, in His wisdom, will otherwise."

Hilda Loeb had been capricious in her lifetime, apt to cancel out what she did. If she bought at the wrong moment, she sold at the right one; if she helped a man she would at the same time broadcast her bad opinion of him. She could afford to and on the whole she finished even because people liked her for herself. This bequest of hers showed the familiar contradictions. It was a nice thought, a good intention that had done harm already. Rose had lost two friends over it and feared she might get too close a look into the natures of some others.

Victorine Gregory was capable of keeping up a pretence of friendship and that would be irritating, possibly disagreeable in view of Sam Swanzy. Cade was another matter, and really regrettable. He was entitled to principles and to distorted ones—provided he didn't exalt them. Now Rose could not overlook them because he would not allow her to. He was pigheaded, which with him passed for strength. Their relationship which had been pleasant and productive would become a rubbing along, with the Self-Help Committee always there to grit up even that.

Rose did not feel she need blame herself. The present deadlock was about as foreseeable as a fall of soot and as tedious to clear up. She might, in the beginning, have chosen the members of the Committee differently and they might have voted differently and the net result might have been the same. She could have chosen better-known quantities but she, too, was entitled to her principles. Once the thing had started to go wrong there was little chance for management, except by preventing a brawl—no one knew better than Rose how overheating committee work could be.

She took a cup of bad coffee which she did not want in order to talk to Miss Havelock whom she saw sitting in a coffee-bar at nearly lunch-time. But that was in obedience to an old-fashioned sense of duty: one should not shirk the unpleasant, however unprofitable it might appear to be.

"May I join you?" said Rose. "Do you mind?"

Miss Havelock minded so little that it was slightly offensive. She said, "I have a train to catch in ten minutes—to a stockholders' meeting in the City."

"I know how busy you are. It seemed sensible," said Rose, "to find out your free dates before trying to fix another meeting of the Self-Help Committee."

"Have there been any developments?"

"In what way?"

"Unless someone has changed her mind we shall waste another afternoon. I can always employ my time."

Rose wondered how. With money? She was not known to be especially avaricious. With getting it, a game for all seasons?

"Mr Cade has withdrawn from the Committee."

"Why?"

"He's sensitive about his church being a beneficiary. It doesn't help us, of course."

Miss Havelock grunted.

"I feel we should discuss it and vote again," said Rose. "Someone may have second thoughts."

"Shall you?"

Rose smiled. "My decision is unchanged, but my mind is still open."

Miss Havelock took a mirror from her handbag and adjusted her hat.

"The Choules woman will do as you do and I doubt if Mrs Betts has had first thoughts, let alone second ones."

"Surely that's a little unfair—"

"Mrs Tyndall has obviously set her heart, so that leaves Mrs Gregory. She's unstable, you might get at her."

"Get at her?"

"To change her mind."

"But she's on your side."

"Mrs Antrobus, I have no side. It is immaterial to me where the money goes. My vote was the expression of an opinion, not a declaration of war." Miss Havelock snapped shut her handbag. She would have done well, Rose thought, to powder her nose which was caking. "I too may resign at the next meeting. The Committee made a bad start. Not surprisingly," said Miss Havelock, "since it's so illogically composed. Mrs Choules is not a committee woman, she'll be a passenger every time a decision is wanted. Mrs Betts plays golf and I've never heard of her doing anything else."

This was not criticism, Rose reminded herself. From whence it came it was betrayal of Miss Havelock's own deficiency. Grotesque, really, that a woman of her size should be so petty—a sport, or economy, of nature to put a small mind in a body as big as an ox's.

"I chose the Committee very carefully, I'm sorry you think it illogical," Rose said mildly. "There were good and sufficient reasons for everyone; I still think they're sufficient, with perhaps one exception. That's what comes of trying to be kind, it really is rather a bad reason for anything."

Miss Havelock raised her eyebrows, refusing to be drawn. Rose said, "Well, never mind, we're often mistaken in each other. It *was* a bad start, but it need be no more than that.

105

We must learn to work together. We can, we're responsible people."

"Opinions vary as to which of us is," said Miss Havelock. Her face then struggled, with diligently curling lip and arching brows, to accommodate an expression which Rose supposed was sarcasm. "It wasn't by any chance me you were trying to be kind to?"

Rose laughed. "Good heavens, no!" She hesitated. "As a matter of fact, strictly between you and me, it was Vee Gregory. I thought she needed taking out of herself."

"Committee work is not a therapy."

"I see that now!" cried Rose. "And I'm afraid it may even be bad for her from a practical point of view. Of course, if I'd known how she was involved I would never have invited her."

"Mrs Gregory is difficult and somewhat affected but presumably she voted according to her convictions. Yes, I would grant her that," said Miss Havelock generously.

"Would you? I wonder. And how much respect should we give the convictions of a woman in her situation?"

"What is her situation?"

"Oh!" Rose subsided, troubled, and began fiddling with her coffee-spoon. "Please don't ask me that."

"I have asked."

"I can't tell you."

"Then you shouldn't hint," said Miss Havelock. "And if it affects the Committee I have a right to know."

"It doesn't really. Oh, I don't know!" Rose was distressed. "The thing is, how much should we expect from her while her standards are so low?"

Miss Havelock looked at her watch. "In two minutes I must leave to catch my train. Either you do me the courtesy of telling me what you're talking about or I shall waste no more of my time on your Committee."

"You're forcing my hand," said Rose, and told her about Victorine and Sam Swanzy.

"Gossip," said Miss Havelock.

"Oh, I know! And were it only that, do you think I'd have repeated it, however you insisted? But my husband is not in the habit of gossiping. His word," Rose said gently, "I do respect."

Miss Havelock picked up her gloves and her nice fox fur. "It doesn't change anything so far as I'm concerned."

"Why should it? If you share her opinions you don't necessarily approve her morals."

Miss Havelock's face mottled to the blemished pink of blotting paper.

Rose sighed. "I have a casting vote, but I would so much rather not use it."

Although Sunday morning church could not have seemed a business potential to Ted Antrobus, he always went with Rose and sat attentively through the sermons, hands in his lap, ankles crossed. He knelt assiduously, stood up promptly, and sang the hymns in a loud voice, but Rose did not know what he thought about religion. She had certainly tried to find out in their beginning. He had given stock answers, dryly, as if to a forward child. She was later convinced that going to church was one of his habits. She noticed his fretfulness if for any reason he was prevented from going: it was the same, exactly, as when he was prevented from changing out of his City clothes and taking his sweet sherry before dinner. Who was to say—of him or of anyone—where habit left off and faith began? An amalgam of the two was the acceptable, the expected, compromise. Religion should be a habit, and so far as Rose was concerned habit might be a religion since it had made Ted Antrobus what he was and since she was satisfied with that.

She said as they walked home on Sunday morning, "I have a feeling Eric meant the text of that sermon for me."

"The poor chap may have meant it for himself."

"In his own mind he's blameless."

"But he can't accuse you of faith without works."

"He disapproves of my works."

"I wonder," said Antrobus, "if you really approve of this one yourself."

"What do you mean?"

"It's a prickly business."

"That's not my fault," Rose said sharply. "I only wish I was always as certain of the right thing to do."

"And you're sure about the wrong thing? You're sure that it's all wrong?"

"I've heard as much as I need or want to about Mrs Peachey."

"Shouldn't you see something too?"

"The idea was that Mavis Tyndall should do that."

"Should do that." Antrobus nodded and dropped her last words over a garden wall.

Rose understood that that would be the end of it for this morning and for as long as she took to raise it again, or for it to come up in the course of anything else.

"You might as well say we ought all to go, all of us who voted against her, and have the poor woman recite her troubles."

"I might." She could tell that he disliked being detained on it. "You've all seen the hassocks."

There was in this absurdity a grain of justice. She picked it out because it contributed to a decision already reached. If she went to Mrs Peachey she might see for herself facts which Mavis Tyndall had not seen or hadn't mentioned, facts which might confirm her own opinion and justify her casting vote. Or she might see something to change that opinion. There was, as she had said, her mind to be kept open.

"Very well, I'll go. No one shall say I did less than I should."

She did more by taking sweets for the children. Now that she had decided, it was obvious: going in itself was the solution. It had been a small matter, she thought, feeling able already to regard it as closed, though full of unpleasantness—the implication being that there was plenty more where that came from. A pity that Hilda's bequest should have provoked it, Hilda had meant so well. So had they all. It was discouraging, to say the least, to get this sort of petty bad where only good was intended.

Mrs Peachey had a flat in a Council block on the wet side

108

of the town, the side the rain came in across the Weald. The new slums, Rose thought, climbing concrete stairs, ten flights between concrete walls, cream-painted and lavatorial. On every landing aprons of damp were driven in through the balcony openings. The building was cold and without being particularly clean smelt disinfected. She met no one, heard nothing except a high Arctic whistling of the wind in the stair-well.

Mrs Peachey's door stood ajar with a broom in the crack. Rose knocked and a tiny girl came out and held on to the broom as if Rose was threatening to take it. It was, Rose, noticed afterwards, her practice to attach herself to something.

"Hallo, dear, is your mummy in?"

The child had lint-white hair and the tender poverty that goes with it. Almost repulsive, Rose thought such thin blue pallor, and surely it was pipe-clay, not ivory her bones were made of?

Something moved on the other side of the door. Rose said, "Won't you tell Mummy I'm here?"

This was the child that Mavis Tyndall was concerned about, the little girl who kept so still. Well she might. Four years of life and she had a look of utter exhaustion, like a delicate weed swamped with rain.

Rose knocked briskly at the door and it swung open, showing her the room beyond, all window and cold stuffy white clouds. Of course it was absurdly high up, at the mercy of the sky. And there was nothing much else to fill it, no curtains, no carpet, just a table, a chair and a drugget over the floorboards and a wooden crate upended to hold books.

"Is anybody at home?"

"No," said a voice.

Rose looked round the door. Behind it crouched a boy, a little older than the girl, with the same lint-coloured hair and the same pallor under a tidal grubbiness.

There seemed not to be anyone else about, but Rose called, "Mrs Peachey?" towards an inner door.

The boy called back, "Nobody at home."

"Where's your mother?"

109

"Gone to the corner."

"I'll come in and wait for her."

She welcomed the chance of seeing without being seen and she could, she thought, also look at these children and they would probably answer questions in their own funny way without her asking them.

But when she got inside her instinct was to walk straight out again. It was the most comfortless place she had ever been in, not so much squalid as uncommitted, the furniture and what served as furniture scattered about, left standing rather than placed. It was bleakly clean and tidy because the signs of living were so few—a folding pram and a cigarette packet seemed to be all.

Rose walked about and the boy followed her.

"I'm Arnold. Who are you?"

"That's a nice name." Rose picked up the cigarette packet. It was empty. So she could afford to smoke—

"Who are you?"

Rose stepped round him to look at the books in the crate: 'The Jury System', 'Litigation and Tenure', 'Governing Slander'. The titles puzzled her, the books themselves were the most solid things in the room and they looked crated up ready to leave it.

"Who reads these?"

"I've seen you before," said the boy. "Oh, my lord!"

Rose looked at him. He affronted her. Children always did, she found their conversation tedious and their hands dirty. This one had a crust round his mouth.

"I've seen you at the church," said the boy. "With Mrs Tinribs, you're thick with her."

"Is that what you call Mrs Tyndall?"

The little girl came and pressed against Rose's side. She wore a pink cardigan shrunk to her elbows, a stale sweetish smell came off her skin.

"What's your name, dear?" Rose touched the child with her fingertip.

"Hers is Flossie." The boy choked with laughter. "Flossie's her name!"

Rose thought she heard a noise from the inner room.

"Who's in there?"

"I don't like you," said the boy.

She pushed the door wide and looked in. On the double bed lay a baby, wide awake, staring at her. Rose withdrew at once.

In the outer room the other children stood silent, watching, and then the girl, drawing close again, took up the corner of Rose's coat, fondled it and made as if she would carry it to her mouth.

"Don't!" Rose brushed off the child's hold. She said to the boy, "Does your mother often leave you alone like this?"

"My name's Arnold. What's yours?"

Rose reminded herself that children need handling and was relieved it was in a figurative sense. She found the scant bird bodies of these two repulsive, the girl particularly. There was something parasitical and sick about her.

"I've brought you some sweets." Rose sat in the chair and opened her handbag. Then she snapped it shut again. "I expect your mother buys you sweets when she goes for her cigarettes, doesn't she?"

"What sort of sweets?"

"Chocolates and jellies."

"Oh, my lord." Grinning, he put his back against the wall and slid down on to his heels. The girl crept to Rose's side, her breath rustling in her chest.

"Wouldn't you like some chocolate?" When Rose held it up and the child stretched out her hand, Rose said, "What's Mummy gone to the corner for?"

Her reactions to stimulus were entirely mechanical. If something was held out to her she lifted her hand, if it was withdrawn she let her hand drop. She showed no disappointment or impatience, she simply sank to the floor beside Rose's chair and Rose was left with the chocolate upraised as if she were making the children sit up and beg for it.

If it looked like that to the woman who came in the door just then it was not the sort of thing she would resent. She wouldn't extend it any farther than the children themselves and they might indeed be performing dogs for all the identifying she did with them. Rose was soon easy on that score but at first she felt at a disadvantage, she even felt guilty.

"Mrs Peachey, isn't it? I do beg your pardon for installing myself, but I wanted to wait and see you and the little boy let me in—" Rose smiled, holding out her hand—"in the sense of allowing me in. The door was open."

Mrs Peachey had the long hair, loosely wound and pinned on top of her head, the provoked and disenchanted mouth, the uniform face of her kind. Hers was the young kind and she was, thought Rose, going to put off being any other kind as long as she could. There was nothing of Denis Peachey in her face, nothing of the children, nothing of anything. Either she had schooled it out or it had never got through.

She took Rose's hand without enthusiasm.

"I'm Rose Antrobus, from St John's Church."

"I don't know anyone from any church."

"You know Mrs Tyndall?"

"Oh, she's from Sunday school." She didn't seem to think it had any connection.

"And our Minister, Mr Cade, has been to see you."

She sat on the edge of the table, still in her raincoat, looking mildly at Rose. "So many people come."

"We like to keep in touch with our parishioners in case there's any way we can help."

"That's what they all come for, to help," Mrs Peachey said softly. "Have you got a cigarette?"

"I don't smoke."

"I'm taking it up. I don't really care for the actual taste, but it's nice when you first light one." She took a packet from her raincoat pocket, broke the cellophane and shook out a cigarette. "This is the part I like." Bending to the flame in her cupped hand she drew with puckered lips and then rounded them to let out a wisp of smoke. "It's like starting a conversation. I suppose I'll get addicted and won't be able to do without. I don't care, it's a private conversation." She gestured without rancour towards the children. "Private from them. I get pretty tired not having anything they don't have."

"Still,' said Rose, "smoking is a costly habit to get into

and unfortunately that's the least harmful thing one can say about it. And there's such a lot to be done with your money, isn't there?"

Mrs Peachey did not concur. She went on puffing and blowing at her cigarette in a diligent mechanical way as if it were something she had to keep going.

"You must find it hard to make ends meet."

"I don't try. What I can't pay this week I'll pay next. People know that, they let me carry over because they know the money comes regular. You might say we're better off."

It would be tiresome if she was going to try to score points. Rose, looking sharply at her, could see no signs of cleverness or aim, except at keeping the cigarette alight.

"No one gave us credit when Denis was here."

"But aren't there things you could do with?"

"What things?"

"You can specify them better than I can."

"For this place? Furniture you mean? What could I do with furniture that I can't do now? I can sit down now and eat my dinner and go to bed—there'd be nothing else to do with it except dust it. I can't draw the curtains and I don't want to, if that's what you're thinking. I want the daylight in and at night I want to look out at the lights—there are a lot of lights from here—and I want to be seen, I want people to see me."

How old was she? Twenty-two or -three she must be to have a child of six, though she looked in her late teens. She gave Rose the impression, even Rose did not think it was arranged, of a premature ending, something started for a sufficient reason and now barely existing because reason and means had gone. Rose was reminded, and it seemed appropriate, of the acute personal poverty of the child, the little girl.

"Nothing for the children?"

"We're all fed and clothed," said Mrs Peachey. "They don't want anything else at their age."

Was it, Rose wondered, only an assumption of negation and only Mrs Peachey's, or did they really have no use for the things that other people lived by and often lived for?

113

"It won't be long, will it," she said smiling, "before Flossie grows out of that cardigan?"

"Who?"

Rose wagged a finger at the child. "You'd like a new coat, wouldn't you, Flossie?"

"For Christ's sake get your facts right," said Mrs Peachey. "Her name's Arlette."

"I beg your pardon—Oh!" cried Rose. "I'm so sorry, really I am—it was the little boy said her name was Flossie—"

"He'll say anything for a giggle." Mrs Peachey bore no resentment, she sat on the table swinging her legs, the cigarette in the middle of her mouth like a whistle. "Nut case, aren't you?" she called to the boy. "Dead or dead-funny?" To Rose's surprise and annoyance they both laughed and Mrs Peachey's was the same laughter, bubbling and noisy as the child's.

She stopped as abruptly as she had begun. "You have to laugh," she said aimlessly and again it was the absence of reason that chilled.

"You don't want anything?" Rose avoided irony, but her eyebrows went up because from where she sat it was a manifestly absurd thing to say. Moreover she suspected that Mrs Peachey did not show herself in the round, she had sides and turned them according to whoever she was with. Whether that was instinctive or expedient Rose had yet to decide.

"Letty's taken a fancy for you." The little girl, crouched beside Rose's chair, put up a hand like a crab. "If people ignore her she creeps after them."

Rose stood up and went to the window. "So money wouldn't help?"

"How much money?"

"I haven't said there'll be any yet."

"Where would it come from?"

"I'm not at liberty to tell you."

"It doesn't matter." Her interest flickered out. The cigarette, too, was finished and she plucked at the buttons on her raincoat. "There wouldn't be enough to buy Denis back."

114

From this height the new estate showed its small begin-
nings: unimaginatively small they had been and the plan,
the tidy garden city plan, had got lost. Rings of red brick
houses snaked round it, shoebox flats overhung it. Looking
down at naked roads, bald playing fields and an agglomerate
of factories, Rose could see neither shape, colour nor co-
existence to make it memorable. At night perhaps darkness
gave it unity.

"Does anyone have that kind of money?" said Mrs
Peachey. "To buy them off?"

"To buy who off?"

"The people who've got Denis. They say he's sick, well
how am I to know when he's better? And if I know, who's
going to listen? They can say it's for the common good and
they could keep him for ever for that."

Queer how it was the inflection of the voice that counted
with Rose. Children whined, complained, excused—'I
couldn't help it, it wasn't me, they made me do it—' and
yet there was no question of sincerity. They felt all that
they were able, and if they pitied themselves they had their
reasons. So had Mrs Peachey. She was no less miserable,
Rose told herself, because she did not keep her dignity.

"I'm sure that when he's better—"

"They'll let him out?" Mrs Peachey uttered a sound from
the back of her throat, but it wasn't laughter. "If you think
that you're simpler than I am. 'Mrs P., we've cured your
husband, he's now a responsible citizen ready to take his
place in the world—' Oh yes, I can hear it, the bells ringing,
the people cheering and the neighbours putting out flags."

"I know it's hard, but you must try—"

"Try what? That's what he did, he tried. He was studying,
see, to be a lawyer and better us. What he really wanted, if
you ask me, was just to be better." She had asked herself
and come up with this answer, and if it hadn't embittered
her it had taken the last grain of sense. "Have you tried
studying at night, Rose Thingummy? Night after night after
night with three kids in the room? We had to keep quiet, I
can tell you—we've gone quiet now—and so did he. He had

to stick his fingers in his ears when the baby cried, I couldn't always stop the baby."

It was irony or justice, whichever way you looked at it, that trying too hard to be better should cause a man to get so much worse. And better than what? Agreed that there was room for improvement, but how much better did Denis Peachey want to be without the natural equipment, poor wretch, to accomplish it?

"He learned that legal stuff by heart." Mrs Peachey gestured with her foot towards the crate of books. "He could say pages off, word perfect, and all they needed when it came to it was one little word to put him away for good."

Rose had an uneasy feeling that Mrs Peachey was goading herself.

"He used to walk about reciting, memorising it, all the way to the bus, in the queue, on the bus and any minute of the day he could get to himself. When people laughed he didn't like it. He was better than them, why should he stand for them laughing?"

"They were showing their ignorance—"

"He hit that bloody old tramp for her ignorance, that bloody, dirty, pissed old whore."

"Please!" But she had not goaded herself to more than the form of words, she was calm, even contemplative and Rose could only say, "The children are listening—"

"They'd tell you the same." Sighing, she stretched and relaxed without refreshment. "Sometimes I think I'll go and start something else."

"Start something?"

"Who would, with me now? I'm past it."

Mentally she was about seventeen, which would be the age when she had her first child and, thought Rose, stopped growing as compensation. Couldn't she see how futile and silly these attempts to shock were for one in her position? If she didn't grow up soon she ran the risk of being permanently retarded.

"Denis took everything. Anyone else would have left me something to pick up and go on with. I'm not specially faithful, it's just that I had it all with him. I'm glad to God I did."

Rose said, using the formula—it wasn't her place to give moral correction, "You have the children, that must mean a great deal."

Mrs Peachey put both arms round herself. "It means that we wanted each other and we got married because he wouldn't have me without. He was as full of principles as a bird is feathers. The kids came, you've got to pay for principles."

"I asked if there was anything you needed—"

"Be a right church that could give me *that*." Mrs Peachey laughed her bubbling child's laugh and the boy joined in.

The question was, just how irresponsible was she? Rose thought she overplayed it, only a crank or an imbecile could be so imprudent. On the other hand she obviously gave no thought to practicalities. Even taking into account the chronic shortage of money, the Peacheys lived bleaker from indifference than from poverty. Of course, some women had no idea how to make a home, with money or without, and some could manage it with a rag rug and a geranium.

The sweets for the children were still in her handbag. She dropped them in the ashcan. Then she made tea for herself and held the cup between her palms to warm them. She felt chilled, which was understandable, the day being cold and the Peacheys' flat so dreary. What was not understandable was the sense of disruption she had, confusion and doubt in excess of anything she needed to feel about the Peacheys.

She was not disposed to look for causes, not this afternoon. There could be several, tiresome and ephemeral. This afternoon she still thought that Hilda's money should go to the church. The fact that the Peacheys needed money was never in doubt; so did a lot of people, more or less desperately, and there was no sign of desperation about Mrs Peachey. She could as well benefit next quarter as this, if indeed whatever she chose to do with the money could be called benefiting. It was inane of Mavis Tyndall to be so sentimental, a childless woman with a fixation about some-one else's children. For that she would hamstring the Committee and sabotage Hilda Loeb's goodwill and testament.

This afternoon, thought Rose, she had confirmed that the Peachey problem was beyond the scope of the Self-Help Committee and should never have been raised in the first place. The interview had shown her a line of argument.

"I put it to you," she said, rehearsing, "should this—or any committee—meddle with emotional problems? We can't help Mrs Peachey until she helps herself. Her problem is her own—" Rose had her eye on Mavis Tyndall—"peculiarly and personally in her situation. She shouldn't be incapable of tackling it, and until she does I don't see her using Hilda Loeb's money the way Hilda or any of us intend. I see her letting it slip away without herself or the children being a penny the better. If we give her the money we must be prepared to forget it, and her. We can look for no positive good and we may do her a disservice." Rose paused for someone—Victorine probably—to ask how she worked that one out. "Having seen Mrs Peachey and talked to her, I'm the last to deny that she has difficulties. The sooner she faces up to them the better. It may be that by the time we allocate the next benefaction she will have made a start and then I should myself move that we give her any practical help we can."

It was a reasonable argument, not that it would convert Mavis Tyndall or Victorine, they were beyond reason. All Rose asked was that Miss Havelock should be swayed.

She thought there was a good chance. She ought to have been satisfied enough to leave the subject alone. But she couldn't get Mrs Peachey out of her mind, there was some-thing ominous about that kind of indifference. She could never have been normal, that was a state of mind, manners and body which she came as fatally short of as Peachey himself. She had harboured and channelled his violence by virtue or vice of simply being, of bringing children into the world, of requiring to eat, breathe and exist. She was culpable, if anyone was for abnormality, as essential as her husband's victim, and much more integral.

The last person Rose wanted to see that afternoon was Victorine Gregory. She arrived just as Rose was trying to contain herself. Rose had discovered a tendency to go to pieces, to turn around to find not only opinions and concepts but the standards of a lifetime quietly leaking. It was frightening. Rose would have panicked if she hadn't held onto the knowledge that it was a temporary reaction: tiredness, due largely to recent frustrations and disappointments. To revive she had only to put right out of her mind this question of poor Hilda's money and everything connected with it: a change of mind, thought Rose, not of heart. She knew she had no hope of achieving it when Victorine turned up.

"I've had the kids and the flower-pot men all day," said Victorine. She came sauntering in, her casualness looked too pronounced. "When I stay alone in that house I start to lose my identity."

"It's your home, it should reflect your identity."

Victorine threw herself into a chair. She looked at Rose as if expecting no great entertainment from that quarter either. "It's all right for you with your blasted committees."

"Yes," said Rose, "one makes friends that way."

"Have you got friends?"

"I think so."

"I haven't, thank God—only you."

"How am I meant to take that?"

"Sue rich-bitch Betts and Mrs Butcher Choules are your friends."

"You're a snob, Vee."

"I've met all the friendly ladies with their claws in each other's backs."

Rose guessed that something particular was provoking this. She guessed what the something was and felt mollified. If the rewards of virtue had to be winkled out it was right that the punishment for vice should be insidious.

"Your back too," said Victorine. "I tell you, it's a closed circle."

Rose recognised a red herring.

"They can't find anything to dig into. They hate that, naturally."

119

You had always to read into her, Rose thought. If her own conscience troubled her, she maligned everyone else; if she wanted information she sought it by discrediting the source.

"Don't you know yourself, Rose?"

Rose said coldly, "The question seems to be do I know other people."

"The principle's the same, the working one, I mean. Prick us and we bleed." Victorine smiled. "That woman's name in *The Water Babies*—Mrs Do-as-you-would-be-done-by—that's sound primitive ethics, but they're no easier to stick to than the complicated ones."

"Would you like tea?"

"Be clean, be tidy," said Victorine, "where it shows, and that's the best anyone can do if the principle's a dirty mess."

Rose was surprised. This had every appearance of leading to a confession, and Victorine must be hard pushed from some more than moral direction if she thought of making one. Rose was also annoyed. She had no wish to hear details of the affair with Swanzy and no intention of taking any of the burden of it.

"Vee, there are people coming to supper and I've things to do—"

"It's the same for all of us—that's sanity. Mine, anyway." She lay in the chair, holding up a lazy hand to Rose who was about to go out of the door. "I like looking at you, Rose, you've got such a lovely crust."

"Don't talk nonsense."

"I long to crack it. So do Betts and Choules. Little Tyndall's the only one who thinks you're solid."

"I'm obliged to her."

"Certainly that's the impression one gets over the Peachey business. There but for the grace of God you never would go."

"No," said Rose, "I never would. And I say so not because of what happened to Mrs Peachey but because of what she is."

"What is she?"

"She's a trollop."

Rose had surprised herself. The word tasted of dirt and was not all, not half to do with Mrs Peachey. It had been declared, smacked down between Victorine and herself, there was no need even to stoop to pick it up.

"Why should I try to identify myself with a woman like that?" Rose said deliberately, "Could you?"

Victorine did not pick up. On the contrary she seemed to let go of something and what was left was not in the least remarkable, in a crowd would hardly serve to identify her. But what was left was Victorine Gregory, the essential. Rose thought, essential to whom?

"I wonder if you and I can work together on the same committee," she said without wonder, and Victorine put her head back against the chair and shut her eyes. She was tired of something, had no hope of it and Rose knew it was neither the money nor the Committee nor Mrs Peachey.

She nodded with approval at Victorine's blank eyelids and went out to the kitchen.

Solange taught me about that sort of thing. Not in words, she wouldn't have thought words necessary. By the time I went to Grieux I was sixteen, I knew about what was crisply called at school 'the reproductive system'. Privately I considered it unnecessarily nasty even for animals. I thought that Nature, said to be so ingenious, could have found some nicer way of propagation, but if we understood aright, the same grotesque and chronically unhygienic method had to be employed between men and women.

I didn't believe we had understood. How could we, confused as we were with Latinised words and textbook diagrams of pollination and genes and the structure of eggs? I didn't believe that the actual mechanics of it were as crude as between ourselves we made them out to be. There was surely a qualifying factor, a saving grace which we overlooked or couldn't know about. I was not romantic, but I liked things to be nice.

I had the sense to keep that to myself. I put up with the whispering and rumouring that went on among the other girls. When they nudged each other about the Song of Solomon I nudged too. I was more irritated than titillated when I read it. The saving grace wasn't there and in the Bible it surely should have been. When they passed round forbidden books what was in them seemed as apposite as the personal habits of the aborigines, of another country and another climate.

My father would have preferred me to go straight from school to commercial college, and I would have liked that. Mother wanted me to finish at a school abroad. She settled on Winterthur House because Solange Marigny was going there.

I still corresponded with Solange, it had become a chore for us both. At sixteen we had less in common than we had at twelve, and although it was still more than we were likely to have in later life it wasn't much and wasn't communicable in letters. I wrote in poor French about tennis clubs and hockey matches and Senior Guiding, and Solange wrote in correct English about clothes and someone called Joanno, a friend of Valentin's.

My mother thought it would be nice for Solange and me to be together again. She had great unfounded faith in the Marignys' shrewdness. Any school they chose was bound to be the best of its kind for its price.

"The French know about establishments, it's the same with restaurants and hotels—go where they go and you can be sure of value for money."

I couldn't see Monsieur le Maître bothering with prospectuses and I did not believe that Madame Marigny, who never finished anything, should be so trusted when it came to finishing her daughter's education. Solange told me later that she herself chose Winterthur House because it was near Basle and Joanno.

I was afraid that being 'finished' with Solange might entail finishing like her. From what I remembered she was more likely to impose her pattern than have any imposed on her. This was not communicable either, not to my mother. She had her way. Father and I crossed a week after my sixteenth

birthday to Boulogne and from there went by the Simplon
Orient to Basle and from Basle by road to Grieux.

Grieux just missed being a place for tourists. It was over
a thousand feet above the sea with a drop to the Belfort
Gap on one side and a step up to the Jura on the other. The
town itself was level, the buildings old but not especially
fantastic. There were some carved eaves and a cobbled
square with a stone bear in the middle and two stout grey
churches. It was sober and tidy rather than contorted and
cute.

My father liked it. I remember his saying it was a gentle
place, perhaps he thought it would do something for me. I
was a big noisy girl, a problem just then. My mother was
constantly trying to get me to walk on the balls of my feet,
to laugh with my teeth together and to cherish myself a
little.

We stayed a night at an hotel with feather bags on the
beds and at breakfast the bread came still smoking from the
oven. I told my father, not for the first time, of my doubts
about this school. It would be too late to complain, I pointed
out, when in a year's time I finished up like Solange Marigny,
and then I tried to tell him what was lacking in her. He
didn't take me seriously when I put all my faith in the force
of her character and none in the combined powers of those
who were to teach us.

As we drove out of Grieux next morning I felt feminine
and defenceless. That was new to me. So was the glassy cold
air, so were the mountains and the goat-bells and the people
with apple faces and woollen stockings, talking their clackety
gibberish. It was packed with foreign potential which at best
was not the slightest use to me and might be downright
dangerous. What were my parents thinking of to send me
to this half-baked place? What did they expect to be done
for me here that couldn't be done in Beckenham?

Winterthur House, named after the town near Zurich,
was nothing special to look at. The special in architecture
and landscape never has impressed me anyway. I don't like
to be bounced into admiration. This was a brown stone
house, dignified in a functional way, with plain shutters and

123

wide eaves to take the weight of the winter snows. I was comforted to see a hard tennis-court, marked out and tidy. It could nearly have been English.

We were taken to the Principal's study. We saw no pupils, nor signs of them. This part of the house was all black panelling and bearskin rugs. There were stuffed stag and wolf heads with papier maché snouts and banks of muscular plants in copper troughs and something which I can never disassociate from Winterthur—a copy of the Laöcoon. I think of it now as indigenous to the place, all that yellow plaster contortion signified.

I don't forget the smell peculiar to the house. It was at once aromatic and bitter, muffling and sharp: the sweetness, I suppose, from the old wood and the polish used on it, the bitterness from the damp soil and the strong dust held in the hairs of the living plants and the dead animals. I am not likely to encounter just that blend anywhere else and it wasn't to be met with in the pupils' quarters. For me it is the smell of Winterthur, of the fields, trees and mountains, the people and everything that happened.

The Principals were the Merkur Kulms. He was Austrian and she German. They were called Dr and Mrs Kulm by staff and pupils. When they received us that first day I saw that he was unimpeachably handsome and that she smiled too strenuously, but as foreigners they were acceptable. That first day it was all aggressively strange and Merkur Kulm made no demands. I was aware of him, as of a vein of richness. I looked at him with some of the dread I had of being left in this place, but I did look. Perhaps I wasn't to see afterwards what I saw then because that was the first time and the only time I was not committed.

He had the luxurious good looks of a cherished creature. He was both solid and graceful, he had a bright academic beard and curling chestnut hair that grew over his collar. My father looked faded and abused beside him.

Mrs Kulm had a broad slab face and black swimming eyes. She spoke English with such care and conviction that her lips were constantly flecked with spittle.

I don't remember what was said. They wanted to show

124

my father the school, but for some reason he was against seeing it. He and I sat moping while they talked and then he suddenly said he was returning to Basle immediately and might I be allowed to walk with him as far as the gate.

He seemed satisfied that the Kulms were qualified to have charge of me. I asked him as we went along the drive and he said yes, absently yet definitely, so there was no hope of getting away. I felt fatalistic after that and my father who was worrying about something quite irrelevant—like how long the parcel post took from England—didn't get any great show of emotion when he kissed me goodbye. He was relieved, I dare say. We always preferred to keep command of ourselves in our family.

I was ready to put up resistance to Solange, but at first I did not need to. She was genuinely glad to see me and she didn't tease, not at first. Winterthur House was new to her also and she had other things on her mind.

I hadn't anticipated so much change in her appearance. There was little enough in mine. I was taller and what my mother called 'filling out'. I rarely bothered to examine my face in the mirror, it wasn't beautiful and it wasn't hideous, so what was there to look at?

"Your nose," said Solange, "still looks damp."

She was a different person. 'Quite the young lady', Mother would have said, and indeed Solange was working at it. Her hair was permed and the perm in those days was inclined to be rigid. Crisp little gables ran levelly and punctually every two inches all round her head. I coveted those waves, my hair was in the mutable state, like two dropped wings either side of my face.

And that strong pallor of hers held good. She did not suffer from colour in the wrong places, greasy sallows or acne. Her skin was dry and white, like a good wine I remember her saying matter-of-factly. She chose her own clothes, they did not do for her what the big-girl dresses our parents put us in did for the rest of us. She looked neither like a full sack tied in the middle nor like a maypole with ribbons.

In style her clothes were ten years too old, yet she never looked ridiculous, she managed to look unique.

I was jealous. I thought I didn't want to look as she did because it was questionable and too fast by the calendar reckoning. I told myself that I wasn't going to be her sort of woman, I already had an inkling what sort of woman that was.

I wasn't the only one to be jealous of her. She did not become popular. She had a small following of people like me whom she called upon whenever she wanted, for whatever she wanted. It wasn't much, it certainly wasn't friendship and we, her cronies, were always ready to ally against her.

There were forty girls at Winterthur, several youngest at fifteen and the eldest, Dutch twin sisters, were eighteen. They and the seventeen-year-olds were known as 'jeunes dames', the rest of us were 'les filles'.

I've since wondered who was responsible for setting the curriculum and conclude that the practicalities were Laura Kulm's and the niceties were her husband's. She would insist on languages, she herself taught us French and German and the literature readings were hers. We had much to assimilate if we were to give the impression of a University education and that, I think, was her ideal.

She was dedicated to the present as a means of bringing about what struck me as a drab, free-for-all future. We were hustled through the classics to ground us for the moderns. There was only a year or two to accomplish it all.

Current affairs was her forte. She told us things that would have constituted an intelligent woman's guide, had we been intelligent women. I forgot, even as I heard, how the Bourse worked and the Stock Exchange and the Reichsbank and I don't know the first thing now about the politics of industry. She was a Socialist, she thought everyone could and should have everything. The first time she outlined for us the theory and practice of her brand of Socialism I had a quite adult feeling that she was only seeing what she wanted to. When her eyes blazed and her bosom actually heaved I decided she was capable of suborning her brain to suit her blood.

126

She was younger than her husband and we wondered what he had seen in her. We couldn't see anything for him in her teased-up negroid hair and coarse skin. She had been a pupil at Cologne University, he an extra-mural Professor of Greek and Latin, subjects unlikely ever to have been of use to her. She was restless and eruptive, she had a powerful crudity. Solange said she was an 'educated peasant'.

Inevitably, so many adolescent girls penned up together carried a torch for the only personable male penned up with them. Some claimed to dislike him because he was pleased with himself, but they were trying to be different. He had reason to be pleased with himself, we made no secret of how pleased *we* were.

Being Viennese provided the operetta streak which charmed and bemused us; being older, but not too old, made him discriminating and worldly-wise. We believed it did, just as we believed he had depths. I think he was an unhappy man and we took his occasional sombre moods for their face value, we were glad of them. Knowing he had depths made us feel cosy, and if we thought of sounding them it was for the sake of what we might do in them and not what we would find.

I suppose when he visualised the girls who came to Winterthur House as future women of the world it was his world he saw them in, hence the emphasis on the fine arts which we had to learn to appreciate by practising them. With many of us it was a waste of time. With me it certainly was. I couldn't tell one note of music from another nor move to it without mixing my feet. As to drawing, it was pitiable the messes I made. He used to say, puzzled and pleading, "But that is not what you see—it cannot—it must not be!"

Even so, he achieved a greater degree of success than anyone else could have done because so many of us impure little virgins were competing for his favour.

Also resident at the school were Signorina Piotta, who taught Italian and tried, in the open discussion sessions, to involve us in astrology; and Miss Gurney, young and shy, who had joined the staff direct from college to take English classes and games. She was a rabbit at games. I remember

127

her as perpetually running to and fro, bleating on her whistle.

There were some itinerant lecturers and some regularly visiting professors, none of them memorable apart from Polichen, the dwarf.

Our quarters at Winterthur were Spartan. Furniture in the dormitories, cubicles and classrooms was minimal. We were not encouraged to spread ourselves—Mrs Kulm's influence again. In the common-room we had some armchairs, hand-woven rugs, a radio and an ugly epergne which we were required to keep supplied with flowers or decorative leaves.

We slept in dormitories of six to eight, with one of the 'jeunes dames' to keep an eye on us. I have always disliked sleeping in the company of other people. At Winterthur I got into a habit, which I afterwards found hard to break, of never quite losing consciousness as I slept. Some of the girls talked and cried out in their sleep. Carème Rossli, the senior of our dormitory, snored like a hunting pig.

Solange had the bed next to mine. She had engineered that: I supposed because she was glad to be with me again. Later I found that she had a better reason.

The proximity of others did not trouble Solange. If she chose, she did not acknowledge them, and until she chose they existed only as a shuffle of air she might feel on her skin. She was naturally lazy. Often in our free periods she would lie fully dressed on her bed, eyes and face wide open, blank to the point of unconsciousness.

I supposed I was seeing her kinship with Valentin, I thought she too was arguing things out in her head. I asked her, curious to know the problems which absorbed her.

"What are you thinking?"

She moved her lips, they were dry from stillness, they had to unseal.

"I am not thinking."

She was bored. There was nothing at Winterthur House that she cared or needed to take trouble to do. The lessons were too easy, the routine too rigid, the company insipid.

Not to me. It suited my temperament and capabilities. I have always preferred order.

"I came to fetch you. Dr Kulm is going to play us some records."

"Amusez-vous." She sealed up her lips again.

I made friends. Four of us came together and kept together during the year I was at Winterthur. They were ordinary peaceable girls—Lisl Norderney, Connie Dace and Mary Sawdell. The odd thing was that being friends of mine seemed automatically to commit them to Solange. Whether we wanted it or not, we four constituted her circle, when she wanted a circle.

None of us knew what to make of her. I found it tiresome being appealed to as an authority. The others would ask, "What does she mean?" as if she spoke a language only I could understand.

"Well, you're her friend," they said.

Was I? Was anyone? I had started to think that there were no friends of Solange, only people who knew her from Adam. But someone, apparently, she took trouble to be with. We had been scarcely a fortnight at Winterthur when she began.

We were getting ready for bed, at nine o'clock as usual. Lights had to be out by nine-thirty. We thought it a childish time. Some dormitories contrived, by a system of sentry-go and water-pipe rappings, to support life for another hour after the Dutch twins, as the supreme seniors, had been round to check on the dark. In some dormitories they read, played cards, ran clubs, ate chocolate, washed their hair and smoked until midnight. Connie Dace liked a good story and maintained that they also drank Fraise des Bois and gagged and bound the girls who got noisy on it.

Nothing happened in our dormitory because Carème, our senior-in-charge, needed her sleep. She was capable of putting the lights out before nine-thirty if we seemed anything like ready, so of course we dawdled. Solange dawdled longer than anyone. It was not unusual for her still be to fully dressed when Carème put the lights out. She was that evening, curled up on her bed, buffing her nails.

Carème called to her, "In one moment I am putting you in the dark."

Solange took her purse bag out of her locker and her gloves and laid them on her pillow.

I said, "Are you going somewhere?"

To my amazement, she nodded. "I'm going out to supper."

"What?"

"Listen, I want you to open the front door and leave it open—at about one o'clock. Yes, I shall not return before then."

"Open the front door? Are you mad? I can't possibly."

"Why not?"

"It's against the rules as you well know. We'd be expelled."

She said something under her breath. I was terrified, I felt as if a pit of iniquity had opened before me.

"At one o'clock." She was polishing her nails again.

"No! I should be seen—"

"You must take care that you are not."

"The door—they'll see it's open!"

"Not at one o'clock." She smiled. "They will be in their beds."

At that moment Carème put out the lights. I was left crouching in the blackness at Solange's bedside.

"I won't do it!"

She did not answer. She knew I would do it, and I knew too. Already the ordeal was weighing me down. I would never, I thought, survive the night.

I whispered, trembling with anger and panic, "Where are you going?"

"That's my business."

"I won't do it unless you tell me!"

She leaned down and spoke close to my ear. "Joanno is coming to take me to supper and to dance—" perfunctory and calm as if she were telling a pestering younger sister.

"You said he was in Basle—"

"Tonight he is in Grieux."

I didn't ask any more. I didn't want to know. Despairing,

130

I crept into my bed. I hated Solange that night. I prayed for her to be caught as she went out, struck down, destroyed. If there was any justice, any defence of the innocent, she would be.

The dormitory was by no means quiet. People were muttering and laughing and settling in their beds. I heard Solange, her breathing and the rustle of her clothes, as loud and clear as the crack of a whip.

I lay on my back. When it began to ache I realised I was hooked stiff with anger and dread. Presently Dutch Rena came in. She woke Carème, who was starting to snore, to say something to her. Rena was laughing. Carème hated being roused, she whimpered and grunted in reply.

After that, the dormitory settled down. I knew when they were all asleep, it was like a tide running out, leaving only me and Solange whom I hated—and was afraid of. Yes, being careful of her turned out, after all, to be fear. I blamed myself. What advantage had she, except my chicken-heartedness? And I had made her a present of that. I had crouched down so that she could stand higher, now I was going to lie flat so that she could walk over me. I would do as she wanted, this time and other times, with everything to lose, because I had put myself into the way. A slow conditioning it must have been. What else? What was there to be afraid of? She was a schoolgirl like myself—like, anyway, in her capacity. There was no more nor less to fear from that.

I was claiming the initiative for my own defeat and managed to keep it a litle while without self-analysis or the fret of redemption. I did not understand then that this was Solange's own game, she would always beat me at it and I was neither equipped nor required to play.

She waited a long time on her bed, perhaps one hour, perhaps two. It was the longest wait I had ever had for anything. I lived it over and over again in discovery and disgrace. I was naïve even for my age. What she planned and my part of it was shocking and iniquitous because it went against my every grain.

I didn't hear her move off her bed, perhaps I'd only

131

imagined I could hear her lying there. She stooped over me and from so much staring the darkness had become semi-dusk and I was able to see that she was smiling. I thought that she used this particular smile a lot on me. It was more than a smile, it was a deepening, as if I brought out her self in her. But there was nothing to be gathered from it, except that she knew all about me.

"Don't go to sleep, Rose." She moved away between the beds and I pushed myself up on my elbow to watch her. She had a scarf over her hair and she wore a dark coat which she must have smuggled into the dormitory. At the door she waved without looking back.

I still hoped. Between Carême's snores I listened for some other sound, some sound of commotion that would mean she was caught. Nothing happened. I pictured her having to hide, making a dash for it, being seen, being chased, being brought back.

Then a car started not far away and roared off in low gear up the road to the Col.

She was gone. A man said, "I'll take you to supper," and she went, though it was an experience we were not considered ready for, not yet. It was forbidden, a progressive culpability starting with the offence of being fully dressed after lights-out and culminating in the crime of keeping company unapproved and unknown to authority in a place unapproved and unknown, for reasons unapproved but soon surmised. And surely culpability ended there and liability began—the innocent's, the green girl's, the virgin's liability to the lust and infamy of men?

It horrified me. I thought how could Solange expose herself to such dangers? She was no fool, she knew what it entailed when a man took an unchaperoned girl to supper.

She knew. I realised that I should never understand her. She was of another race, another creed, another sort.

She hadn't troubled to arrange the pillows to look as if she were still in her bed. It was I who did that, and when the clock chimed one I crept down and unbolted the front door.

I don't know what time she came back. She was just a

thickening of the dark beside my bed. I had been dozing and dreaming but I knew she was using the smile when she said, "I would do the same for you, Rose."

That was the first time. She went again. And again, and each time I swore I would not help her, and she went just the same. Once it was past two o'clock before I unbolted the door. I knew I was going to do it but I hoped she would come back and find herself locked out and have to wait, and I hoped it might scare her, alone in the cold and dark. It was only me who waited and was frightened enough for both of us.

I reasoned that if she were caught she would inculpate me, not from spite—it took trouble to be spiteful—but because she had no conscience.

Towards the end of term they found the door open one morning. I had opened it. Solange was unconcerned. Hadn't I said I would not let her in—wasn't I too nervous, or too tired? Naturally she hadn't relied on me, she had made her own arrangement. It had been complicated, but it had worked and she had not needed to go to the main door. How could she dream I would change my mind? As she understood me, it was a matter of principle, she did not expect me to change that.

When we were interrogated I had to lie. Solange could speak the truth and listen to me lying. She was the only one who knew, but I heard through my own voice and thought everyone else heard through it too.

One of the kitchen staff was already suspected of staying out at night. Nothing could be proved, but fault was found with her work and she was dismissed.

Solange did not go out at night again that term. She resigned herself to Christmas at Winterthur—the holiday was too brief to allow us to go home. It was not the exhaustive festival we made in England and I was thankful. I hadn't much peace and I didn't feel entitled to get or give goodwill.

Merkur Kulm was a failure manqué. I think he would have

had a more compatible brand of unhappiness if he'd been left with his own might-have-been's, if he hadn't been mercilessly fixed in a candle-glow at Winterthur. I know it's easy at this distance of time to add people up, but it's not within my power to be particular. There's no necessity. Everyone must amount to so much, more or less, in a final analysis. This one of mine cannot be checked, let alone corrected: I must take what I can find.

I find that Kulm was a man who would be private and she, Laura Kulm, was a king-maker. That would be enough, neither criminal nor very comic, and I would not have looked further, I would not be looking at all if Solange hadn't shown me.

The school was the Kulms' kingdom, his to reign over, hers to police. She had a precise idea of what she wanted for him and she prevailed because he had no idea what he wanted for himself. It was his undoing that we all had our own ideas of him. Ours were mawkish, yet I fancy Laura Kulm's provided for and to some extent depended on them. It must have suited her down to the ground to keep him hobbled among schoolgirls who could not come near him intellectually or emotionally. That way she secured for him both the prerogative and limitation of royalty. No doubt the balance was painfully kept: to us in our ignorance it appeared to be tipped. We wanted more than a monarchy for Kulm, we wanted a beloved despotism.

There were two seasons that winter. Outside was the feral cold and a grandiose backdrop of mountain and forest. You could sooner walk unawares amongst a brass band than amongst that. After the raw bloomy winters of home it was meretricious. Within doors was the private season which was more than a season, it was an expectation of life. We did not doubt who gave it to us.

I see now how insufficient Kulm would have been alone. He could never have established himself against the ructions and disruptions of forty adolescent girls. He would have gently proffered what he had to give and we were at the stage when it needed to be imposed.

As I knew him he was a mixture of men, incomplete and

biddable most of them. I say as I knew him because I think that without Laura Kulm he would have been faithful to his shortcomings. I can imagine him being content with them. What he gave Winterthur, what she obliged him to give, was essentially his own. I put it as a private resource which would have kept him comfortable and comforting at whatever level he chose to drift to. The struggle was to stretch the private resource to a public fund. They both had to work to do it.

It was Laura Kulm who made the laws and punished us when we broke them; it was she who watched us, her black eyes swam everywhere. They couldn't see into our souls, but they looked into places which we considered private. The state of our finger-nails and the backs of our stockings were near personal; as near, we thought, as hare-lip or acne. Such things ought not to be remarked on in public.

If we laughed we were empty vessels, if we ran we were tomboys, if we gathered more than two together we were geese.

"She thinks she owns us," we said. "She wants a box of tin soldiers."

"Shooting us down is more fun."

"What's it to do with her if our suspenders are twisted and our face-flannels smell? She's no right to go sniffing them."

We tried to mimic her—"You may be sisters under the skin, but you have a choice of company this side of it."

"It's no use, you can't spit as far as she can—"

"What's it to do with her if I fix my hair with a rubber ring? It's more hygienic than hair-ribbon."

We were women enough to resent a woman's thumb over us, but what really disturbed us was the thought that Kulm was under it too.

"Why doesn't he put her in her place?"

"He's too kind."

"It's not kind to let her get above herself. He should exert his authority, after all, he is the Principal."

"So is she."

"He's a man. She's forgotten that."

We decided that he was himself to blame.

"I'd surely like to remind her."

Solange said, "Children, how do you remind a woman that her husband is a man?"

We said coldly that we could show our own regard for him. But of course we already did that, it was expected of us.

We thought that if she could see Miss Gurney or Signorina Piotta acknowledging his superiority she might remember it herself.

Solange said, "Any man can be a man among women."

We left it there because we couldn't see how he was ever to be a man among men at Winterthur.

Is studied kindness less kind? At the time I wasn't to know that Merkur Kulm was keeping to pattern. I would have been humiliated if I'd thought he was doing what was required of him. Although he was a warm-hearted man can I be sure—could he, even?—that he actually wanted to do what he did for me? That he would have done it without Laura Kulm's blueprint? I can't be sure. The sweetness has dried out, I see myself as another score to be made. The truth, I suppose, being six of one, half a dozen of the other. There's no place for that in a final analysis.

Kulm had an uncritical affection for music. He delighted in everything from hill-billies to Bach. Nose-flutes, Welsh choirs and symphony orchestras—he tried to show us the best in each of them, equipping us for a world where we would cultivate our pleasures. I don't think he visualised our needing to cultivate much else. Yet he could never have known the world he was at such pains to make us ready for and I doubt if anyone had—it did away with such a lot that has always been with us.

Not with dancing: we were expected to dance as an obligation of citizenship. Only physical deformity could exempt us. As I have said, I was big and maladroit, the dancing lessons were a trial to me and I considered them a waste of time.

"I shan't do this sort of thing after I leave here," I told Kulm.

"Do not pump your arm so—You mean never to dance? That's entirely absurd."

I said, "Obviously it would be better if I stood still."

"Why? You are not a tree."

"Only the Rose," someone said.

I despised dancing and I wouldn't have cared about looking a fool at it, but suddenly I felt written off. I felt I would never make a woman, not Merkur Kulm's sort of woman, and suddenly I didn't want to make any other sort.

It was a shattering discovery. I was shattered. I stood staring, probably I had my mouth open—it was dry because my heart was beating in my throat.

He said, "Miss Rose, it is just a little turn with the feet—so," and I tried but of course I couldn't do it, certainly not at that moment. My turn went into a spin and they all laughed. Kulm called out sharply, "Take partners for a waltz," and turning to me asked with ceremony and no mockery for the pleasure of this dance.

It was only what was required of him. To me it was a beautiful nightmare. I trod all over his feet while he smiled and supported me as if I were a vine. What with the clumsiness of my feet and the giddiness of my heart I expected to fall right over. I had to cling although his touch shrivelled me. Once his smile froze and he murmured into my ear, "Please do not *shove*, Miss Rose."

When the class was over I tried to get away by myself. The others wouldn't allow it, they came round like cats circling another with a strange smell on its fur. They made me out to be a bit of a clown.

"Why Rose? He was asking for the pleasure, wasn't he?"

"She's nearer his build than anyone else."

"Do you think he likes big women?"

"They made a handsome couple," said Solange.

I was afraid that they would see how wide open I was. I thought I had as much chance of hiding it as of hiding chicken-pox. This was the first time I had been delivered over to someone else and as it turned out the experience

137

did approximate to a chronic and febrile sickness. It shook me out of a quite sturdy optimism and for a long time after I left Winterthur I could not trust myself because there had been intimations, to say the least, that there was more to me than I needed or cared to have. It was an awkward age and of course it passed, but there were times when I not only felt diseased, I felt disfigured.

Love, in this crude form, I had to try to keep whence it came—underground. There was no room for it at Winterthur. I hadn't known there was room in me for such splendours and miseries. Thank heavens I can't remember them in detail, they would be painfully absurd.

I dreamed, not always unashamedly, and shuddered to think what the others would have said if they knew. I suffered from the contrast between their idolatry and mine. My wants were imprecise and Kulm was the source of them all. I doubt if he could have supplied them all because sometimes I was one negative ache for everything under the sun—the state, I suppose, of just being in want. I had to listen to the gossip of those who manoeuvred to touch him and bribed Carème, a flagrantly bad artist, to paint miniatures of him which they put in lockets and albums. He was common property, in the exchange I saw him lose a little every day and every day I recouped the loss. His was an acutely physical presence that had commandeered me during the moments we danced together. I remembered him somewhere deeper than my heart and with parts of myself that until now had served mundane purposes. My skin was still apt to fire all over as it did when he had touched me, and either my blood ran too fast or stopped altogether—anyway I felt dizzy. Then there was my nose, shamelessly recreating, so that I was aware of him as one animal is of another. I was hungry to smell his clothes, his soap, his cigarettes.

I worried about that. It was different from anything the others felt and I didn't think it could be nice. Coming from me it might indicate something I should have to suppress in later life.

I was apprehensive of Solange more than anyone. Her

138

own affairs never completely absorbed her, she had a knack of seeing the germ of other people's at a glance.

It wasn't easy to dissemble because the joke now was to pretend that I was his favourite. I dared not let them suspect that I pretended it too in secret and dreamed abysmally stupid dreams in which he took me away and held me, not dancing, just holding me and kissing the palms of my hands.

Solange said it was unhealthy the way we all fastened on Kulm, it was bad for women to be without men and for me particularly bad. When I asked why she said because I was 'très sensuelle' and might become perverted. I knew she was just passing the time, she often did at my expense, but of course I got frightened and when she said I should meet more men I overdid it and cried out, "How can I—here?" as if we were in a nunnery. She told me, though not conclusively, that I was a fool. She was dangling a line, I think she had a whim to involve me with herself.

That was the last thing I wanted, so I left my foolishness for granted. I was reminded soon after of what I would have been involved in.

Less than a month after the new term started the six of us from our dormitory, excepting Carême who, as the senior, was interviewed alone, were summoned to the Principals' office.

Mrs Kulm was waiting for us. She was angry. As we went in she looked searchingly at each of us, not to find so much as to confirm what she already knew. I suddenly felt sick with dread. Surely I was the only person who could make her so angry? Somehow she had guessed how I was thinking and what I was thinking about her husband. She was going to denounce me to those I might have contaminated with my sinful thoughts. She was going to rub me out like a dirty mark.

Of course I looked guilty. As a girl when I blushed I swelled, the skin of my face felt ready to burst with blood. She said to me, "Which of you has left the school by night?"

I grunted as if the wind had been knocked out of me.

"Miss Rose Tedder, was it you?"

I don't know why—hearing my name brought out like that

139

perhaps, at any rate it was purely mechanical—I said, "No, Mrs Laura Kulm," before I could stop myself.

She gave me a blazing stare. It killed my upsurge of relief and rekindled another anxiety.

"Then who was it?"

I dared not look at anyone. We all kept still and Mrs Kulm's mouth, never pretty, broadened without humour like a monkey's.

"I need not remind you that leaving the school thus is violation of the rules, in my opinion to the extreme, and punishable with expulsion. This I promise you, mesdemoiselles, I will discover—" she spat the words with care, "I will break this practice!"

Solange asked, "Why must it be us?"

"I am reasonably assured," Laura Kulm said bitterly. "Which one, or ones, I shall wait to discover."

"Wait?"

Solange might not be that sure of her ground, but she knew she could always walk somewhere else.

"I shall lie in wait," said Mrs Kulm and it seemed so simple that the moment collapsed. She could never do enough, I thought, to harm Solange, but it could poetically or scientifically or wantonly turn back on herself. I didn't at any time fancy her chances.

"Make no mistake, I shall watch, I shall not ask someone else to do it. One night, ten nights, a hundred." She stared at me, I think she had decided that I was the one. "I never sleep until two in the morning. It will be enough."

Solange would be smiling. I knew the sort of thing that amused her without always knowing why. I was afraid of her smile, it wasn't broad and grinning, but sometimes I saw it like the Cheshire cat's, without her, without her face or her lips, just the air smiling.

No one else spoke. There was obviously a great deal that Mrs Kulm could have said. She must have thought we were not the people to say it to. She warned us again. She was determined, she said, to end this situation, and looked as if she wished it was a matter of ending us too. Then she

140

dismissed us. As we turned to go she cried, "I will lie in the door!"

We looked back to see her standing, drawn up to her full height—she was short and dumpy—her head thrown back with an assumption of dignity. She only managed to look defiant and I suspected that if browbeating wouldn't do it she simply did not know how to put the fear of God or herself into us.

When we got away, the others asked what it had been about and they asked us if I was the one who could tell them.

"It's not me," I said, "whatever she thinks."

"Then who is it?"

"What did she mean about lying in the door?"

Mary Sawdell turned to Solange. "It's you, isn't it? You're the one who goes out at night."

Solange smiled. "Where would I go to?"

"I can see how bad it would look for the school," said Mary gravely. "Of course you wouldn't think about that."

"I'm always thinking about the school. What else, when I am always here?"

Someone said cautiously, "Whoever it is won't be able to again because Mrs Kulm's going to be on the watch."

"Lying in the door!"

"That's a figure of speech—"

"Don't be sure," said Connie Dace. "She worked day and night to get this place started—I don't know about him but I guess he worked days anyway—and she won't let anything happen to discredit the school's good name. Rena told me they have a whacking great bank loan. I guess Mrs Kulm will lie down any place to keep that paid up."

"Naturellement," said Solange. "She is a peasant."

I used to wonder how I could ever be finished when I left Winterthur. Half the time I didn't know myself and for the other half I didn't like what I was getting to know.

The curriculum, too, confused me. Whose world was it? To my way of thinking there were only two possibilities, though even at sixteen I didn't expect it to be all music and picture galleries or all money and politics. There was bound to be something of everything and a finishing school should surely help us get our proportions right.

We weren't being helped at Winterthur, we were being loaded with irrelevancies in the hope that enough of them would stick to give us sense or sensibility. To me, the worlds were quite personal and wildly different and there was no question which I wanted to live in, music, picture-galleries and all. Laura Kulm's wasn't spread for us like her husband's, she kept it to her classes and it was about as rich and heady as a glass of liver salts.

I wrote to my father telling him that I was more unfinished now than when I came, that it was a waste of money to keep me at Winterthur, that I was unhappy and wanted to come home. When I read the letter through it sounded querulous. He would wonder between the lines, he knew me better than to believe that waste of money and lack of finish would make me unhappy. I carried the letter about for a week. Nine times out of ten I could not bring myself to post it. At the tenth, unnerved and homesick, I dropped it in the box.

I felt no better and no less about Merkur Kulm. The feeling was in my heart and my head and in places I hardly reckoned to exist, except in a medical sense. And whatever it was—'love' I still called it—was alienating as well as corrosive. I felt transparent, it isn't too much to say that I felt unclean.

Everyone knows the formula, if not from direct experience, from fiction—the fact that one can find it in magazines evidences how commonplace it is. I've seen it in print, with and without pictures, for the world and his wife to read about, the same tragi-comic and, as I thought then, unique affair. I suppose I'm lucky I can say it's been unique within my own experience. Outside adolescence it might be less painful but a great deal more shaming.

Being the magnetic centre at Winterthur, Kulm made the place electric for miles around for me. He had his own problems and as a kindly man would have been disturbed to know how much depended on the crooking of his finger.

Luckily for him, he was completely unaware—with me taking fire in front of him, burning up yet unconsumed like the bush for Moses.

Speculation as to who could be breaking school was never rife. The suspects were Solange and myself. We were uncommunicative, nothing further happened and no one knew for certain if Mrs Kulm was actually keeping watch. The subject turned into a joke. Only Carème respected it, out of officialdom. Every night as she switched off the lights she said, "No one is to leave the dormitory except for natural causes," and five minutes later we could all have stamped out and slammed the door without waking her.

Not long after Mrs Kulm's interview I awoke one morning and saw how restless Solange was, turning on her pillow and murmuring. She seemed distressed and I had never known Solange distressed, even in her sleep. I leaned across to look.

She had make-up on. It was smudged into the pillow, lipstick that made her mouth purple in the clinical daylight, and crusted powder, and her lashes sticking black on her cheeks.

I guessed at once what it meant. She was mad or doomed or invulnerable but I had to try. I shook her.

"Wake up!"

She looked at me from the bottom of somewhere. I got out of bed and bent over her and I could smell where she had been. A bitter-sweet hard smell it was, foreign in an inimical way.

"Take that stuff off your face!"

Her eyes were glassy and almost foolish. She wouldn't see, she rolled away from me with a groan.

I wiped her face as best I could with a damp flannel.

She was the last to get up that morning. She had no breakfast, I think she was sick.

We had a free period from seven till nine in the evening. We were expected to make up discussion groups, listen to intelligent radio programmes and read the classics. It was

Mrs Kulm's method to cram us with culture at every point of entry hoping that we would retain the quintessential. What we mostly did was gossip and play dance music.

I waited until evening before I spoke to Solange again, and then I walked her up and down the corridor so that we could be private. I said I knew she'd been out again the previous night, she was a fool, she'd be caught, I said, sooner or later and it wasn't going to be my business but this once I was warning her. She asked why, what did it pay for, and I must have said something about owing it to myself because she pretended not to know what that was about and said surely no one would think I'd been letting her in all the time? She would explain that it had happened infrequently— Once! it had happened once! I cried—but she pointed out that we might not be believed because Mrs Kulm would naturally not care to think that her rules could be so easily broken by a girl, one girl, going in and out as she chose.

I knew I had to draw the line then, she would panic me just as far as I let her. We were in the passage giving on to the hall. At that time of day the hall was regarded as part of the Kulm's private residence, pupils were not expected to intrude there. I walked away into it without another word, intending to get out through the conservatory door.

I should have known Kulm would be there at that time of the evening, but for once I hadn't been thinking of him. Seeing him—he had something pretty, a pot of camellias, in his hands—caused me the shock of glory I always had at sight of him. I was dismayed too, because I had no business there. But he smiled as if I had been invited.

In my exaltation I felt the world dropping away from me and when he looked past me at Solange who had followed me in I did not grudge her anything. It was intoxication to be so suddenly in his sight, his private sight, without twenty others diffusing it.

He did not reprimand us, it seemed to me he was glad we were there. He talked about the flowers in the conservatory: 'beautiful freaks' he called them, and he said we would see true flowers, gentians and hyacinths growing wild in the mountains. I knew it was right to prefer simple things and it showed how right he was, but I thought the hothouse blooms were prettier.

Of course I didn't say so, I didn't say anything, I just hung on his words. Solange said she liked to have things when other people didn't. She picked the head of a camellia and threaded it into his buttonhole.

I couldn't have done that, not as she did, as if she were both saying and bestowing something. I wouldn't have dared even to pick a flower and I was jealous of everyone and everything with the privilege of not caring.

Kulm looked thoughtful and talked about the best things in life being for everyone. He's Socialist too, I thought. I disliked the idea that any of Laura Kulm should rub off on him.

Solange was bored. She walked away, fingering the plants and when her back was towards us he took the camellia out of his buttonhole. With the point of his gold propelling pencil he dug a hole at the base of the camellia plant and buried the flower.

"Miss Rose," he said, tamping down the soil with the flat top of the pencil, "I have this morning had a letter from your father."

I was watching him. I could appreciate the significance of the ritual, I wished Solange had seen it.

"Yes, I had one too."

There was a middle door in the conservatory. He closed it and we were cut off from Solange. She turned round, I think she watched us, stroking her own cheek with the tip of a great fern.

"Do you know what he has written to me?"

"No."

The last thing I wanted was for the Kulms to suspect that I had asked to be taken away. I had made that very clear but I didn't know whether my father had respected my confidence.

"He asks for a report on your progress." Kulm put the pencil in his waistcoat pocket and looked at me. "I am not sure what I shall say. You have been with us only a little while."

I can still remember corners of his face, the triangle between the cut of his beard and his lower lip and the perfect nib of bone at the end of his nose.

"I sometimes think you are not happy, Miss Rose."

"That's not the point, is it?"

"Not?"

I expect I sighed. I was living, had lived—at that moment I felt immeasurably older than him. "One can't expect to be happy."

"Of course not. One cannot expect, one must *be*." He seized my hands, I thought he was going to make me dance. "It is a duty, Miss Rose, a sacred duty. All else is stupid sin."

I said, "I don't believe we are meant to engage in the pursuit of happiness."

He burst out laughing and pushed my hands back at me.

"What do you know of it? Or of anything that is not written on the blackboard?"

It occurred to me, without titillation this time, that I didn't altogether know him. Experience was allowed for, was in fact required, but not jealousy of it. And here he was, shutting me out before I had got a foot in the door, using his remembrance of things past as unfairly as if he had used his man's strength against me.

"There is nothing to pursue, nothing to run like a mouse. We are not meant to chase, we are meant to achieve. What else is perfection for us but happiness for a minute of time? We cannot be long perfect and we cannot choose when the minute shall come."

I hadn't known him harass a backward pupil, but he was practically stoning me with words. I suppose I went wooden because he sighed with patience regained.

"Why aren't you happy?"

"I didn't say I wasn't. According to you," I said miserably, "I wouldn't even know."

"That was not consistent, I was being resentful of what you have not. Forgive me, forgive all of us who think that to be young is to be happy."

He was inviting, coaxing me to mock him, doing what he

146

was required to do. This was the old mixture, Laura Kulm had mixed it herself and she knew it would work.

He asked again why wasn't I happy and I mumbled that perhaps this was not the right school. That was stupid because of course he wanted reasons, specific ones. Why wasn't Winterthur right? What was wrong? He was thoroughly alerted. I was sure that if he kept looking at me so piercingly he must see the reason staring him in the face.

"Not right for me, I said. And I only said perhaps."

Nevertheless, he insisted, obviously some aspect of Winterthur did not come up to my expectations. Which was it, the standard of education, the system, the régime or the accommodation and what, precisely, were my expectations? I must appreciate that for him as Principal it was essential to know.

"It's nothing really, just a feeling—" I blushed and tried to slip past him. He put his hands on the bench behind me so that I was restrained without being touched.

"Is it a question of personality? Someone you are not in sympathy with? Miss Rose, is this so important? Is it not bound to happen throughout your life that you cannot love your neighbour as yourself?"

He was so close I felt I was getting drunk on him and I must have looked likc a fish, a mullet, open-mouthed and scarlet.

"But perhaps you are worried because it is one of your professors? Is it someone you cannot wish should instruct you?"

I cried out truthfully that it wasn't that sort of feeling and untruthfully that it wasn't really any sort, just a feeling, and then I knocked his arm aside and ran to the door.

"Miss Rose!"

He spoke softly, though as I remember it there was an edge in what he said.

"If the school does not appear right for you could it be that there is something to be learned? Could it be that you will not be happy until you have learned it?"

147

I did not leave Winterthur House before my course was finished. I had a further letter from my father saying that he was satisfied I was in good hands and should give the school a fair trial—his idea of a fair trial being another six months. If at the end of that time I still wanted to leave he would be prepared to reconsider. That had to suffice for me, though I speculated what his reaction would have been had he known my reasons for wanting to get away.

The strong and lavish winter has taken over in memory. I can't always separate it from the spring and summer that followed. I remember the heat of the sun and a vulgar profusion of wild flowers, but I am more likely to coincide everything that happened at Winterthur with the snow. The snow seemed eternal, and looked it. Only the black ribs of the trees demonstrated how pure and nearly almighty it was. When it went it uncovered a secular world of forests, fields, villages and roads, identifiable and human. The sound of melting snow, the shrillness, was never out of the air and still when I think of Winterthur there is this sibilance as of something extra and private going on.

The seasons decided to some extent what games we played and how we spent our leisure hours, but Winterthur was our kingdom and its frontiers were never really crossed. Not for me. In the holidays home was narrow as a dream and I waited to get back to reality.

That rarefied existence was real. I think most of us were satisfied with little, provided it was a little of the right thing and provided we could believe there was any amount more to come. There were a few for whom Winterthur was like living in a paper bag, but for me everything outside, my own life included, was incidental, and after that one attempt I gave up all thought of going back to it. Having made my gesture I accepted defeat: I welcomed it.

I gave myself up to my emotions. Being denied other outlet they tended to heighten and romanticise my consciousness all round. Kulm was the sum of existence, everyone and everything at Winterthur had a smattering of his glory—Miss Gurney and Polichen and Signorina Piotta.

Even Signorina Piotta's stars. They were an establishment

148

superstition. We blamed or consulted them in the same spirit as we threw salt over our shoulders, there was nothing to lose and there might be something to gain. On the occasions when one needed to enlist all the powers it was better to invoke some that weren't than leave out any that might be.

There was more to it so far as I was concerned. I like to think—I still do—that not everything is left to chance. I would sooner suppose that the scope of my life was delimited aeons ago by the solar system than that it is a matter of luck or just my own uninspired doing. Hearing Signorina Piotta talk about ascendancies and conjunctions, crediting one man's misery to Saturn and another man's joy to Jupiter comforted me like a spoonful of syrup comforts a sore throat.

It is difficult now to define that place and how it could contain us. At the time we weren't even aware that we had needs, though from Merkur Kulm we certainly had the impression that they were being met and that they always would be.

I cannot define, either, what he did for us. He wasn't a particularly good teacher of music or dancing—why had he given up Greek and Latin to teach us these pastimes? What mattered to him? The school? Laura Kulm? I suspect he had lost sight of whatever it was and had to concentrate on what mattered to everyone else. Had we all been collectively unhappy and the gift of himself not enough, I don't think he would have known what else to do. His was a lateral talent for heartening the timid and promising the bold. One can have a talent for being or for seeming to be. Where others were adequate at best his talent was to seem so much more. Since Laura Kulm exalted and exploited it probably it was the only one he had.

At Winterthur we were a mixed crowd and might have been expected to be constantly living down each others' foreignness. We lived with it instead, we were cosmopolitan to a skin-depth, a matter—no more, of admitting and celebrating each others' holidays, saints, talismen and attitudes. Co-existence did not much increase our understanding but

149

it created the blithe and mildly scatty atmosphere which we believed to be worldly.

And the Kulms did their best to bring us out into their approximation of the world. Between them they reckoned to provide the essentials for the sort of people we were likely to become. It was as important to be able to amuse ourselves as it was to label our governments and identify our classics. We had 'evenings' once a fortnight when we danced to an energetic little orchestra borrowed from the town band. Connie Dace said she could hear the 'oompha, oompha' in every waltz, tango and foxtrot they played. I couldn't, I have never had any ear for music.

One afternoon the substance of Winterthur leaked out during, of all things, a history lesson. We were in high summer then, pink dust crept across the tennis-courts and to hear waterfalls we needed to go high up into the mountains. We didn't, we were too lazy, the heat exhausted us, we fanned ourselves with our books, we dabbed on Eau de Cologne and Witch Hazel.

It was the end for us all, though to Solange it was probably no more than the end of another day or night, circumstance or habit. And why should I suppose it was the first time for Kulm? Or that there wouldn't be another? Laura Kulm was invincible, she wouldn't admit a defeat in the family.

I can see a funny side to it now—stuffed as I was with novelettish nonsense and urgent and ugly longings. I hadn't been warned about the pangs of growing up and I refused to accept that we shared the principles of the farmyard. I was forever putting those longings behind me. Every time was the last time I would feel like that. I was always newly converted, but I managed to keep private the vision I had of myself calcined and matured by suffering and it was snuffed out that afternoon.

I suppose there's some recognised specification for a dwarf, some minimum height a normal man must grow to and perhaps Polichen wasn't a dwarf. People and places get glorified at a distance of time. If I were to see him now as he was then I might see just a man of under average height, shortsighted and none too clean.

He lived in Basle and came to Winterthur House every week to lecture us in history. The lecture was, in fact, his sole method of instruction so far as we were concerned. We were not expected to interrupt him with questions, and if he questioned us it was to illustrate his conviction that we did not know what he was talking about. He had a poor opinion of our mental capacities, he told us frankly that we were being required to use what we hadn't got. Women, he maintained, had other talents, and although he did not leer there was no doubt about the *double-entendre*. It disgusted us, coming from him.

All the same, his lessons were interesting. History came to us tuppence coloured, his colour. He had a monopoly of the past and he made it live on his terms. Perhaps it was a way of compensating himself for his size.

We tolerated him, as I daresay he knew. We were big even about his penchant for touching us. He was restless and wound-up, he always had to be moving as he talked. In humour, mock anger or sheer necessity he would every now and then put his hand on one of us. He had no preference, it depended who was near at the time and we accepted it as some sort of compulsion, like a nervous tick. Although we didn't care to have his tobacco-brown fingers pressing into our arms and his big head nodding at our shoulders we thought, 'Poor Polly, it's as far as he can ever hope to get.'

It was unusually humid that afternoon. There was a storm coming, it arrived the same night and the thunder and the rose-red lightning seemed fitting after what happened earlier. We were all feeling the weather, Polichen had been prowling since before classes began. When we arrived one of the shutters was flung back and he was padding in and out of a slab of sunlight. He wore the same suit winter and summer, we excused it because of the trouble he must surely have getting anything to fit. He hadn't even left off his waistcoat and his face shone like lard.

We flopped at our desks. We were at a low ebb, I felt it was the lowest ebb possible to sustain life. The sun forged in at the open shutter, putting a finger of heat on us all. The cicadas chirped endlessly and made me homesick for the sparrows chirping through the rain. I longed for some English rain.

We waited without enthusiasm for the lesson to begin. When Solange went and pulled the shutter to it was a relief. Although the air still packed us in it was under wool, not brass.

But Polichen said, "Why did you do that?"

"To make the room cooler."

"I did not hear you ask my permission."

"It's for the general comfort."

"I am in charge of the general comfort, mademoiselle."

Solange inclined her head politely. "Your pardon, Herr Professor, I thought perhaps you could not reach the latch."

There was a rustle. No one laughed. Polichen hooked his thumbs into his waistcoat pockets. There was time for what Solange had said to be said again. And again. And no doubt it was, in his mind. Then he twitched his elbows and began to talk about the First French Republic.

His method was to split open major historical events and shell out the facts for us like peas from a pod. Whenever we laughed about him, we qualified it by adding that he had a brilliant mind.

The heat did not make him lethargic. He never seemed able to relax. If he sat at his table he immediately got up again. The chair was too high for him, it amused us to see him fish about with his toes when he lost contact with the floor.

He trotted to and fro, talking all the while, touching our desks, picking up our pencils, leafing through books. He licked his thumb and rubbed at a mark on the wall. In his way he was bursting with something and we rated his pride or his entitlement to it so low that we did not think of anger.

"The queen—" he was talking of Marie Antoinette— "was enceinte at the time. Enceinte—" he turned on Mary Sawdell. "What is that?"

Mary wasn't terribly bright and she had been half asleep.

"Enceinte—from the French," said Polichen. "There are

152

two meanings, one for a castle, one for a woman. What would it mean, miss, if I should say you were enceinte?"

Mary only suspected the word. She blushed when somebody giggled.

Polichen pulled her hair none too gently. "If I should say that, it would mean a miracle. For you a miracle, an immaculate conception—" Laughing, crouching, holding on to his knees, he turned to Solange. "But not for you, eh, mademoiselle?"

Solange was as surprised as the rest of us. I could see her trying to put two and two together. Polichen set his hand on the back of her neck and brought his face close to hers. "It would not be such a miracle if you were enceinte. Au contraire, it would be something of a miracle if you were not."

"Please." Solange made a frank gesture of distaste and tried to push his hand away.

"Please? Indeed you have pleased certain people if I am not mistaken."

"You are mistaken."

Of us all she could least endure being touched. As she moved her shoulders, Polichen tightened his grip. She tried to stand: he held her, smiling with clenched teeth.

We didn't know what we were seeing, the others knew less perhaps than I, and I felt as if a very wrong record had been put on the gramophone. In the hot vacuous afternoon a little bit of private history was being made.

"Why do you fidget, mademoiselle? You cannot pretend you have not been held by a man before."

"A man, yes—but not by a petit monstre."

She had gone white about the lips, there was no blood in them and they quivered—not, I thought, with anger, but from necessity. She felt sick.

And Polichen was not what we had been used to, bulking no bigger than an undersized child, indifferent to us except for those moments of touching, without pride and with only his one conceit of shelling out the past. He was undersized still, but all there was of him was overcharged with a very present, personal fury.

153

He had this raw spot about his size and we were seeing it pressed upon. He lived in Basle, he could have come across Solange and her friends and been scandalised. Whatever she went to Basle for it wasn't to behave herself, and for all we knew the immoralities of history had made Polichen a phrenetic prude. And he was, as we all were, under the weather that afternoon. But I don't think that was enough, I think something else had already happened, or Polichen thought it had.

He held Solange by the neck and the more she objected the more violently he held her. He was not a powerful man, he did not scruple to use both hands and to brace his knee against the desk.

She too was a bit beside herself, she tried to beat him off like a swarm of flies. He kept reminding her, panting with courtesy, that we were in the middle of a lesson, that he would be obliged if she would stay, that he would say something to interest and enlighten her.

The rest of us just sat there, the record on the gramophone was the wrong record for us all. We listened because we didn't know how to stop it and because we suspected—anyway I did—that it would get worse.

Then Solange broke free. It was an ungraceful movement for her and we rose to our feet. Someone cried to her to run, we wanted it to finish. But Polichen ran too. As she snatched open the door he pulled her back. I cried out and so did others; some of us were frightened, even those who were enjoying it felt that any moment they might not be.

Left to Polichen it might have left off there. Solange, feeling herself caught, became quite frantic and instead of turning to fight his hold fought round her, fought the air. She was so much taller than him, it looked as if he were trying to pin down an overlarge butterfly.

He was only trying to stop her leaving the classroom. Her frenzy had abated his, he must have realised that it ought to be kept to ourselves. If Kulm had not come neither would the moments which none of us enjoyed. Except perhaps Solange because I never understood how or where she found enjoyment.

Our relief was almost corporeal, it fixed Kulm at the other end of the pole from Polichen, the wholly fine and large end. Kulm looked startled, as well he might at finding one of his professors struggling with a pupil and the class bunched round, watching.

He asked if anything was wrong. Polichen said no and Solange said except that the Herr Professor had gone out of his mind.

Kulm considered the rest of us, scared but eager as a crowd witnessing a brawl.

"Should we discuss this in private?"

Polichen said there was nothing to discuss. He had always understood that how he conducted his classes was a matter for his discretion.

"Tell him to let me go." Solange plucked at her fingers as if they were sticky.

Kulm said that Mademoiselle Marigny might safely be released and Polichen replied that it wasn't a question of safety, even for him. He would be obliged if Dr Kulm would not think it necessary to intervene. Dr Kulm would surely agree that to be taught history, to be taught anything, a pupil should remain in class, subject to the teacher. Dr Kulm would surely appreciate that if authority was a nice balance how much nicer it had to be in his, Polichen's case—

"I can't stand any more of this," said Solange.

She looked quite desperate, trembling, her lips pale and her fingers dusting themselves in panic.

"Release her," Kulm said sharply.

"She has made a name for herself—did you know?"

"I order you to release her."

"A bad name for this school—"

Kulm knocked off Polichen's hold. It was a sudden movement and Polichen's hand, flying up, struck off his own glasses.

There was a hush, we were shocked and glad. Everyone looked at the glasses lying on the floor. Polichen was so short-sighted he wasn't sure where they were. He stooped and groped for them.

Kulm himself bent and picked them up. "I'm afraid they're broken."

Polichen fumbled with the spectacles, trying to join the broken halves.

"I'm sorry, Herr Polichen, I apologise. Of course I shall pay for the repair—"

"It's of no consequence. I have others. We will resume the lesson." Turning, Polichen stumbled into the wastepaper basket.

There was a murmur and a laugh.

Kulm said, "If you wish to fetch your other spectacles I will take charge of the class."

Polichen stood behind the table, there was something chilling about his stillness, he who was forever fidgeting about.

"Go to your places," he told us. "Everything is history but everything is not memorable."

Solange turned to Kulm. "I must speak to you—" but Polichen said that she was wasting time, time he was contracted to teach in. If she was not contracted to learn he asked her to do him the courtesy of sitting down while he went through the motions.

"I can't stay here!"

"In the circumstances, Herr Polichen, I think she might be excused."

"In the circumstances?" It was apparently an insult, the last required straw to break his self-control, although I fancied he was himself snatching at and throwing on the straws. "What circumstances? The ones you have engineered, the ones God inflicted on me or those which this girl has brought on you?"

Kulm frowned. "Whatever this is, I think it is not history."

"Permit me to judge that!"

"I insist we adjourn the class before discussing it."

"Permit me to decide that." Polichen's voice, always high-pitched, turned shrill. "I do not require anyone to carry the spoon to my mouth—contrary to appearances!"

"Herr Polichen, remember yourself—"

156

"I do, though not so highly as you remember yourself, Herr Doktor. Which is strange, when one thinks of it!"

Solange appealed to Kulm. "Can we forget he is small if he himself cannot forget it?"

Polichen tried, with his wet eyes, to focus her. "I have a good memory and I have good sight with my glasses. Yes, at two in the morning I see like a fox. Like a mouse if you wish, like a flea! I have seen your name in the dirt, Herr Doktor Kulm and the name of this school. I have heard you remembered without charity—"

Kulm turned his back. "Please go with me to my office," and I think Polichen might have gone if Solange hadn't said, "Don't leave us, Dr Kulm, we're afraid, we're all afraid when he's like this."

Kulm looked round. "It has happened before?"

To our knowledge it hadn't, but we felt that we had never trusted Polichen and the point, surely, was that it had happened. I felt no great scruple about giving a wrong impression, though I was uncomfortable about the way Solange bowed her head without replying.

Polichen swore that she was a liar, we all were. He swore that he had seen Solange in Basle at a time when she was supposed to be in her bed. There were places where a woman of discrimination would not go, he had seen this young girl in them, this 'fille-de-joie' he called her, and in his towering rage gestured, dazzled, at the rest of us. For all he knew we were in the habit of creeping out to men at night. If the eye had not seen the brain could surmise.

Solange said he was mad. By then Kulm was himself having misgivings. I remember how he touched the dew of heat off his upper lip with his silk handkerchief, his face openly trying to make itself up one way or another, whichever way was best suited to the situation.

There was us, of course, we did complicate things, but at the time I assumed we *were* the situation and was confident that Kulm would handle it.

Polichen demanded an apology from Solange for saying he was mad.

Kulm said patiently, "We will consider the matter closed until classes are over."

"Closed? Is it nothing for a teacher to be insulted by a pupil during the conduct of his class? By such a pupil?"

Solange appealed to Kulm. "I was held by the neck like a dog. It's kindness to say he is mad, so why should I apologise?"

"Will you not tell her?" cried Polichen.

"This is neither the time nor place—"

"What other time, what other place? Are you indifferent to a gross dereliction of discipline?" Polichen was fond of tall words. "Is it your intention they should all take a leaf and spit upon me at will? Oh indeed—" he dashed the water from his eyes—"anything is permitted here." He went close to Kulm, plucked at his lapel, raged with his finger-tips over Kulm's waistcoat. "I have seen such things here as only a flea should, a flea between husband and wife, Herr Doktor. But this flea was under a stone—" blindly he pushed his chin into Kulm's chest—"in the garden—this flea has a voice and can speak—"

"Restrain yourself!" Kulm's face was scarcely his own. It was blunted and moist as if the stifling air of the classroom was melting him.

Polichen crouched, bending his knees, twisting his neck, squinting up, pretending to look at a giant.

"God made you big and your wife has made you bigger. Bigger with what? Greek? Latin? I have some Sanskrit in my little finger—enough for a doctorate—" Polichen hissed up at him—"*in nubibus*, Herr Doktor, for here we shall surely not be asked for more."

"You are not yourself, Herr Polichen—"

"Am I not? Yet I am more than you. More than a little music, a little dancing, a little whoring." Polichen, on tiptoe, seemed to be trying to spit the words into his face.

Kulm said nothing. To us it looked as if he was not even parrying, just bending his neck.

"Herr *Doktor*—" it blistered on Polichen's tongue—"if I am to be insulted and my word despised it shall not be here.

I shall choose who looks down, I am not to be ridiculed by women or by a woman's doll."

We waited. There was so much for Kulm to do. Probably most of us favoured violence—I wanted Polichen destroyed with a word, a single withering word, not a blow. Whichever way it was done we were eager for it, none of us doubted that this was Polichen's zenith, that he had been allowed to go so far in order to fall the harder.

Kulm said nothing, did nothing except look over our heads at a piece of vine caught in the top of the shutters.

We were all naïve, and I was naïve enough to wonder why Solange should smile at Polichen and why he should appear to crumple before it. He had been given the last word, it still rang round the room. It was unnecessary and defensive of him to cry as he blundered to the door, "I have better to do than teach history to strumpets!"

PART FOUR

"You're going to tell her," said Sue Betts, "in so many words?"

"I've already said I didn't think we could work on the same committee."

"What did she say?"

"Nothing."

"She'll keep stalling if she thinks it bothers you."

They were in the church, doing the flowers for the week. Rose had brought Baronne Tonnaye tulips, white narcissi and branches of double cherry from her garden. The blossom was in balls which would open by Sunday but were still fragile. It irked her when Sue too briskly disentangled the sprays.

"That's Vee, permanently off-centre."

"She's aiming for the soft private centre," said Rose bitterly, "and she thinks she's located mine."

"There's nothing personal in it. She's made so she can't go straight."

"Straight?" Rose looked up from bruising the stems of the cherry.

"Well, direct. With her it's method and no matter."

Were the stupid, Rose thought, like the pure in heart, to them all things stupid, all things pure?

"I don't like the method, but make no mistake, there's matter too. Vee's an intelligent woman." Rose propped the blossom in an altar vase and stood back to judge the effect. "She'll make a show but she won't obstruct me." Rose was ready for her to try: the Committee meetings gave scope and audience for Victorine's witticisms, she might be as unwilling to part with them as a comedian with a good stooge. Rose was quite ready. If a request for resignation went unheeded there was a consideration—Rose would not say 'pressure'—which could be drawn upon and which even Victorine Gregory, intelligent or stupid, impersonal or

163

malicious, could not afford to ignore. Rose had only to say, naming no names—certainly not Swanzy's—that there was a rumour among the Committee members which she had been obliged to hear, a feeling which she, Rose, did not share, that Vee should be kept out of public life. Especially when it was associated with the church and reflected morals. Hypocrisy, Rose had only to say, was what the Committee feared to be accused of. "Who to invite in her place is what's bothering me."

"There's no problem, surely? I could name half a dozen right off."

"Name them."

"Jane Frossart and Beryl Kinnear for a start—"Rose had known that she would start with her golfing cronies—"and Peggy Vine and Kate Putnam. They're all sensible."

"You mean they'd think as we do." Rose began to settle the narcissi as a background for the tulips. "They would, wouldn't they? It would be said I'd picked myself a quorum. I want to be fair, Sue, and I want to look as if I'm being fair. In any event, Jane and Beryl are too new to the parish and Peggy Vine's abroad half the time."

"What's wrong with Kate?"

Rose said patiently, "Kate's too right. She's Secretary of the W.I. and we both belong to the Townswomen's Guild." Sue was now absently picking buds off the cherry. Rose twitched it away. "And don't propose Mrs Parradine. Her husband and George Choules are at daggers drawn."

"I wasn't going to. What have you against the Colebrook sisters?"

"Nothing, except that there are two of them."

"Honey, I declare you're being obstructive."

"I'm being careful. I'll think of someone, but it won't solve the immediate problem. Vee's vote on the Peachey question will have to stand."

Sue Betts groaned. "That name again! My stomach grabs every time I remember what Mrs Choules told us."

"There was no need," Rose said sharply. "It was irrelevant and sadistic."

"What made you pick her for the Committee?"

"She'll be useful. It's as well to include someone in the trade on a welfare committee."

"I wouldn't like to have her take up golf."

"She's not the type."

"We're not getting the type any more." Sue took out a pink face tissue. "They all come."

"So Ted was saying. People like Sam Swanzy."

Sue raised her eyebrows. "I wonder he told you that one."

"What do you mean?"

"Did you cotton on? That was clever of you. I had to have it spelled out and then I didn't laugh enough." She swept up the stubs of cut stalks with her tissue. "Those jokes are too technical for me."

"What jokes?"

"I must say I didn't think Ted would repeat that sort of thing to you. Hartley says I'm broad-minded if you take 'broad' as a female noun. I shouldn't talk this way in church—"

"Why shouldn't he tell me? Vee's a friend of mine." Rose said tartly, "I'm one of the few people with a right to know and if I'd been told sooner we might have avoided this impasse."

Sue Betts had scarcely any eyebrows of her own, but she pushed high her two pencilled arches and in an oddly guarded way opened her eyes wide. "How and all, honey?"

"I wouldn't have invited her on to the Committee. Personally it doesn't matter to me one iota." Rose carried flowers in a white plinth vase to set on the altar. "Vee has the right to manage or mismanage her private life without me sitting in moral judgment. But if indeed she is so mismanaging her private life I have to question whether she's likely to lead a responsible public one."

Rose, before the altar, twitching the tulips to rights, felt she had put that quite well. She was vexed when Sue Betts said, "You surely aren't thinking that old thing about Vee and Sam Swanzy?"

"Old?" Rose swivelled round. "How long has everyone known?"

"What's there to know?"

165

"Unlike Mrs Choules," said Rose, "I've no intention of filling in the details."

"Could you?"

"What do you mean, Sue?"

"In my opinion it's just bad-natured gossip and I give Vee the benefit of the doubt." Sue Betts spoke carelessly but with a pin-pointing stare. "So do you, don't you?"

Rose recognised that this was an engagement, if not a prepared pitfall. Vee herself had said, "There are claws in your back too—"

"Privately I do. Publicly I can't."

"Honey, people are such worms."

She had gone and Rose was picking up her things to leave when Cade came in from the vestry.

He said, "I thought I'd find you here." It seemed to afford him discomfiture more than pleasure. He stood looking at her with something so patently on the tip of his tongue that Rose disposed herself for one of his appeals, irrelative and usually unanswerable.

He waved at the flowers. "They're nice."

"Yes, I like the Baronne Tonnaye. Tulips are such a hard flower, they do best in these soft colours." She waited, so did Cade—for impetus, apparently. He still had his hand extended and his mouth ajar.

The opportunity given, Rose pulled on her gloves. "I must see about lunch."

Cade shut his mouth and swallowed whatever he had been going to say. It went down lumpily and the voice he was reduced to was his pulpit—announcements and church business—one.

"We're starting a fund—" he corrected himself—"an *emergency* fund for the hassocks. It will have to run concurrently with our standing appeals—Famine Relief, Pensioners, and the therapy garden at Overcourt. Oh, and there'll be John Dance to pay for the yews, he's too poor to do it for nothing. But people can be made aware and we shall press ahead as from now. We wondered if something

166

might be arranged in conjunction with the voluntary societies—"

"Who wondered?"

"Mrs Tyndall and I." Warned, but unprepared, he held tighter to his ceremony. "She has been good enough to go into this with me. She herself is organising a bring-and-buy sale and undertaking to contact people who will set up the usual money-raisers. She is also investigating the possibility of a new plastic manufactured, I believe, by a cousin of hers—"

"*Plastic* hassocks?"

"They would be cheaper and well-nigh indestructible. I suggested we enlist the women's guilds through you. The church has been so much your concern—"

"Has been?"

"Is," said Cade quickly. "Of course it still is."

Rose smiled hard. "How nice to know that Mrs Tyndall is such a comfort."

"She has been most practical."

"Don't be misled. Fundamentally she's not a practical woman. Her heart rules her head—she has such a full heart."

"This is our church, we all kneel in it to pray. I don't see the necessity—I never have—" he hesitated: there, at last, was his appeal—"for a clash of personalities. We must supplement each other's efforts—"

"And the fund may even grow if there's no prior claim on it."

"Once donated, the money could not be diverted."

"Not to some vital human need?" It did her injustice, but she could not stop herself. "A retarded child without toys, perhaps, or a criminal lunatic's wife without saucepans?" His face goaded her, it was the stricken standard face, not venturing more than standard dismay. "We all kneel down, all of us who take time from our own affairs to come and pray. The unbelievers can stay standing. They've chosen to."

Outside the sun was shining. A shaft of tumultuous dust was launched between them through the Baptistry window. Cade looked across it as from some high, dry, privileged place. Was he going to tell her—it would still be standard—that prayer was acceptable however it was offered, provided it came from the heart, knees could be straight, hands could be working, eyes wide open to temptation?

"Are you a believer, Rose?"

Ready for the banalities, she answered sharply, "I try not to confuse sentimentality with faith or carry those who are able to walk."

He smiled as if he too had been ready. Rose felt her anger rising to its true, its native occasion. Sue Betts had only disturbed it, the origin was earlier and now was here, the origin was Cade.

"I also try," she said, "not to mistake conceit for conscience. I never have thought it within my power to put the world to rights."

"Fear is the worst part, fear always is so much worse than the realisation."

"Fear?"

"Would it be so terrible," said Cade, "if you were to feel something?"

I am in church, thought Rose, I must remember that. She looked at Cade; she thought, despise him—you must—he is not worth more. He has merited nothing but vexation, I see now that he is not the origin.

"What are you saving yourself for? Rose, can you be so prudent—" he was frankly mystified—"so rash?"

It was a gap which she had no intention of bridging for him. Only he would be stupid and presumptuous enough to ask her. She picked up her basket.

"If you are going to preach, Eric, I suggest you wait for Sunday."

"I do remember—" he was, as usual, unable to leave well, or ill, alone—"that you believe some are chosen, to be suffered but never to suffer because they have too great a capacity for it, not being—" he was getting it down, in all earnestness, to layman's level—"what you might call reinforced, like the many of us. It was your contention, wasn't it, that such people are sacrosanct, never to be plundered or in any way destroyed, except peacefully, by the grave?"

"Is it a sin," said Rose, "to be peaceful?"

"Immune from wars, pestilence, earthquakes, all acts of God?"

"It might be one of His more logical acts."

"Liable neither to sickness, sorrow, nor bereavement? Apartheid," said Cade, "by special dispensation, from the ills that flesh is heir to?"

"There's no one here to appreciate that kind of humour."

"I'm not being humorous. I can't condemn what I can't altogether see." The golden dust broke over his head as he poked urgently through it. "I want to see, I'm trying to—"

Rose was walking away down the nave. "It doesn't matter whether you do or not."

If Ted Antrobus brought home a business worry he did not air it until it was a *fait accompli* and occasion for worry was past. His method of induction, of acquainting one world with another in so far as was necessary to balance them, was to disallow all immediacy. By the same token, when he brought home a business pleasure, he hitched it on to anything but business.

Now that he had carried through a long-negotiated link with the French Balto Company he was pinning his pleasure to the trip to Paris which the deal necessitated.

"I've a fancy to see that old witch at Croix-Rouge with daffodils in her baskets. Drenched, of course, she keeps a Flit spray full of water."

He sipped his sherry. For him the moment was complete, he would be lucky if any on the trip amounted to as much. "All the times I've been to Paris, but never in the spring. Isn't there a grain of truth in every cliché?"

It was to be a social event, cocktails at the Balto office followed by dinner at the Tour d'Argent. Antrobus was pleased that Rose had been invited.

"It will be a refreshing change from routine for you."

"From parochialism."

"Balto have their executive hive in one of those bankers' streets off the Rond Point, behind the Théâtre Marigny. Very dignified and solid, one would think they'd started hiring cars when Haussmann was building. Their money is all over France, they don't tie themselves to passenger vehicles as we do. They hire out heavy-duty equipment, trucks, tractors, diggers, cranes, drilling-rigs—they have roots. I think we can look forward to a nice little celebration."

"Marigny?" said Rose.

"The theatre. You remember it, a pretty little place on the grass. Played and owned by the Jean-Louis Barrault Company."

"It would be nice if we could have some time to ourselves."

"We might go the day before the party or stay over a day afterwards. Which would you rather?"

"It doesn't matter."

"If you're thinking of shopping, the party is on Tuesday but the big stores close on Monday. It would be no use going a day early."

"No."

"Are you thinking of shopping?"

"Perhaps."

"What else?"

"Nothing else."

Antrobus shook his head. His smile irritated her. It was indulgent and she was not used to being indulged.

"We had better go on Tuesday morning. The notice is short enough as it is."

Naturally whatever was nearest looked largest, but he was seeing it as a question of scale—sometimes ants were almost human too. He tilted his glass to watch the sherry slip in sweet curves down the side.

"Should I make an anonymous gift to the church for favours received—the Balto agreement is quite a favour—and asked—we want a safe journey, don't we? It would be an appropriate gesture, though barbaric. Just a modest sum, say fifty pounds?"

And what was this, thought Rose, this refusal to appoint values except on his own scale, but a kind of parochialism? If his skin was his parish, could there be any getting away?

"The occasion has been priced." Antrobus smiled. "Why pay more?"

"You needn't pay as much. I understand the church is being provided for."

"It is? By whom?"

"By Mrs Tyndall," Rose said bitterly.

He would not wonder how, he did not wish for details. He said, "So it's settled?" and added to her resentment by being frankly prepared to drop the subject for good.

"Nothing's settled until the Committee meets again."

"But there is no deadlock?"

She might have told him that the deadlock had ceased to be important and then he would have asked what was worrying her and she was unable and certainly unwilling to tell him.

"I haven't changed my opinion about where the money should go. I still maintain it would be doing the woman a disservice to give it to her at this stage. Even though that makes me a monster."

When he raised his eyebrows she cried, "To Eric Cade it does."

"You all appear to have lost your sense of proportion over this business. It has brought out—" he paused—to modify his words, she thought—"a new side of you."

"Perhaps you too think I'm a monster."

"Don't be ridiculous."

"There's nothing new, I hope, in my refusing to go along with sloppy thinking and mawkish sentiment. Of course this thing has been exaggerated, it's been laboured. I'm surprised," said Rose. "I wouldn't have believed intelligent people could be so petty. I've tried to be sensible, but when everyone else is making mountains it's hard to remember we're dealing in molehills."

"Not molehills." Antrobus closed his eyes. "Hassocks."

For him, that epitomised it all, her part as well as the rest. He needed neither to deny nor ignore, he was simply

171

unaware of any further dimension in her, though she was beside him, within touching distance, though they spent some third of their lives together. She knew, moreover, that he would wish to be unaware: he would, with relief, have chosen to be.

"I could give chapter and verse for all of them. The person who surprises me most disagreeably," said Rose, "is Eric Cade."

There was a faint recession, a withdrawal, from under Antrobus's closed lids which she recognised as his preparation for tedium. She had seen it before when people did not realise that he had finished with a subject. She herself was usually ready to finish or relinquish it at his moment. Now she felt a disproportionate dismay.

"I thought he was a sensible man, I reckoned on it."

Sensible was the word if one gave it its due, full measure. 'The same', she could have said, 'I thought he was the same'—because ultimately there was only one way to be. "He's not even adequate. Surely we're entitled to expect something slightly above average from a man in his position?"

Antrobus had not expected anything. If he had claims they were not laid in that quarter.

She said furiously, "Sanctimony and a sheep's heart is all he can bring us."

"But he's by way of being a shepherd. His flock expect a certain affinity with themselves."

It is a convention still to look for more. Convention is a kind of order too and if I go to church out of tidiness that's as good a reason as habit and a better one than caution.

What did I look for? From the man of God a little godliness, I suppose, though I learned as long ago as Bonneval that the Infinite does not rub off, even on those nearest.

He should at least know where he stands. It isn't as if he has a choice. He would like to have—he would choose to be a victim. It would be his surety. Suffer and you are

absolved, you need not answer. He would like to be cruci-
fied, then he would know he was right.

I don't know if I am right. I know I could not bear to be
wrong. I shouldn't survive, I should simply cease, have to
turn my back. Events have shaped and not rough-hewn me
and I must take it to mean that I amount to more or less
than the other sort. Or to something different.

I am as I have been turned out, with no provision for
violence. With no necessity for it, either.

Is it irresponsible to have had a quiet life, anti-social to
want one? As to wars and acts of God, must I strip myself
raw for the whole world?

The other sort does not require anything of me. Certainly
not my vicarious participation in their affairs. It would be
futile to borrow from a burden without being able to take a
straw off the weight. Besides, they are self-sufficing, capacitated one way or another.

Solange was not just capacitated. I think of her, herself
immutable and immune, as pulling violence out of the air,
out of petty virtues and out of prayers. Perhaps she enjoyed
it. Perhaps it was the only way for her to live.

She was young, she might have changed. She will be a
woman of my age now, surely she won't want to start anything? Did she ever want to? Perhaps she was the catalyst
that brought it on, perhaps she still does and it breaks over
her like a dry wave.

"Is that what you want to do?"

"Yes," said Rose, "that's what I want to do."

"You won't have much time."

"It shouldn't be too difficult. Her father was a well-known
lawyer and they had a flat at Neuilly."

"Why haven't you tried to find her before?"

If she said because it hadn't mattered before he would
feel obliged to ask why it mattered now.

"It's a whim."

"You don't have whims."

"I have this one."

173

"An old school friend?"

"I want to *know*—" Meeting his gaze, she amended quickly, "I'd like to know what happened to her, that's all."

"Too much, probably, to track down in one afternoon. How long since you heard of her?"

"It must be thirty years."

Rose understood that he did not wish the day in Paris to be pre-disposed, he wanted it left to turn out as it might—at this moment of euphoria he could see it turning out very pleasantly—"She may be dead—" but he was unlikely to make any positive fight to retain it. "If she is, of course there's an end."

"What's the connection?"

Rose was surprised that he should ask, although she appreciated that the last thing he wanted was to be told.

"Connection with what?"

"It has the smell of principle." He drained his glass. This was the moment, precisely by the clock, when they reckoned to finish their drinks and go into supper. "If a few preliminary enquiries could be made we might discover whether the person you're looking for is in Paris."

"Now you think I'm being sentimental—"

"The Balto people might investigate so far as the present where-abouts are concerned."

"How could they? Why should they?"

"Because they are in Paris and because I should ask them. They have a man, Bonnetante, for the public relations side. This should be within his scope."

"Bonnetante? Good Aunt? What a funny name," said Rose. "Would he mind, do you think? This is a personal matter, nothing at all to do with your business."

"I shall say it has charitable connections."

The affair was well organised. They were met at Orly by Bonnetante in one of the Balto cars and driven to the Place Vendôme. Their hotel was Balto policy too, Antrobus said. He defined it as the art of giving always a little more than

174

was expected, even though it might mean supplying a little less than was needed.

There was certainly a little more at every turn in the hotel. White gloves and a coachman's cockade for the commissionaire, gold fretwork cages for the telephone booths, a kiosk selling chocolate and tiaras and in the lifts inlaid wood panels of Eastern scenes. And, as Antrobus pointed out, the telephone booths were less than soundproof, the kiosk was locked and there were no floor indicators inside the lifts.

It worked another way: the place was baroque, tarnish and a little dust would have made it blowsy, but there was instead a sense of a great deal being done, devotedly, out of sight, to be served up with a flourish, with ice, or the manager's compliments. A sense, in fact, of an expensive hotel. More expensive, Rose decided, than they would have chosen for themselves.

"You will not lack comfort here," said Bonnetante, and his tone inferred, "whatever else."

He was a young man with a vast body, a behemoth in a hopsack suit. One leg of his trousers would have clothed Antrobus. He appealed to Rose, "Comfort is the important thing?"

"On a short visit," agreed Antrobus. "I should think they do you pretty well here."

"Indeed it is much in favour with visiting firemen." Bonnetante beamed, inviting them to share his pleasure at the phrase. He ushered them into the lift. "If you will permit I shall see if they have forgotten anything."

At the doorway of their room Rose exclaimed, "Why, it's a suite—"

"I thought yes, a sitting-room. Mr Antrobus will have business papers to read." To Rose he politely drew down his chin into the solid folds of his neck. "And ladies like to retire."

The sitting-room was a study in tapestry and fumed oak. "It is the Windsor Suite," Bonnetante said proudly. "Do you feel yourselves at home?"

"My dear fellow," said Antrobus, "it will be difficult to remember we're in Paris."

Rose hardly had time to put down her handbag and take off her gloves before a waiter arrived with tea.

"I thought yes, the four o'clock." Bonnetante detained the man while he checked the tray. "With cold milk and arrowroot biscuits. It is all here."

"How very thoughtful of you," said Rose.

"It is my pleasure. Should there be anything lacking, but anything, acquaint me, please, immediately." He backed to the door, his suit ebbing and rucking on him like the hide of an elephant. "I will leave you to take tea. A car will be here at seven. Until then, au revoir."

At the door he lifted his hand and seriously twinkled two fingers at them.

"He reminds me of Oliver Hardy," said Rose when they were alone.

"Do you begin to see what I mean?"

"It seems ungracious when he's so painstaking."

"The point is, we could have done without this—" Antrobus gestured at the room and the tea-tray—"whereas what I do need is an hour's hard talk, figures supplied, with one of their people, one intelligent, unequivocating man off the road."

"You could ask for it?"

"I could, but I wouldn't get it." Antrobus lifted the lid of the teapot. "Mystique you're bound to encounter in any business and with Balto we're not even consanguineous. Blood will be thicker than oil."

"Teabags," said Rose, "with a label to hang outside the pot. The milk may be cold but it's been boiled. I think I remember where we are."

"The smell's no different. Less acrid, perhaps, than in winter. I wouldn't say it was loaded with anything indefinable—anything I wanted to define, that is."

"I didn't like to disillusion you," said Rose, spooning a flake of fat off the milk, "but whenever I've been to Paris in the spring there's been a gritty wind."

Oddly enough, Rose herself supplied a little more than was

expected—more, anyway, than she had expected of the Balto premises. As Antrobus had described, they were in one of the seemly boulevards having neither cause nor incentive to move with any time other than their own structural depreciation, and that would be leisurely, judging by their ample set on the ground, their slabbed and stone-faced walls and the ecclesiastical spread of their doorways. Outside, the chestnut trees too had stood a long time and the pink blossom looked ill-advised, already it was browning and being surreptitiously dropped.

Inside, Rose was at once aware of a familiarity with the place without the slightest practical knowledge to justify it. In some purely atmospherical way she had been there before. The curious appeasement, the sense of arrival, had always come to her inside that door.

She indulged it at first, luxuriated while the introductions were made: here, she was moved to think, she would meet no enemy. That was feasible, of course, since she was unlikely to get to know any of these people well enough to make friends or enemies.

As it happened she had no opportunity even to find out how much of Cavour, Balto's managing director, was face value. At first sight he impressed, a mighty, angular old man, impeccably turned out, with the curling beard of an Assyrian. His looks did not reflect his capabilities, whatever they were.

In shape his wife was a reversed 'S', carrying her breast and buttocks like offensive weapons. She was vividly powdered and pegged out with jewellery. She spoke no English, to Rose's careful French she adapted her face like someone listening to a badly-tuned radio.

There were a dozen guests, regional agents and their wives, the Company's lawyer and a silent boy in a rusty tuxedo who was thrust forward as Cavour's grandson.

Rose could have picked Bonnetante's wife out of any group. She was a saffron blonde with his same soft debility. She was pretty in an unhealthy way and already getting on for drunk.

There was pressure on people to drink. Wedged behind

the bar, Bonnetante was filling glasses, young Cavour was plucking them empty out of hands and off the tooled-leather top of his grandfather's desk. Rose held on to hers, she had taken only a sip. It was not her wish to cloud or colour her own sensibilities. They were rosy enough, at this stage she needed to clarify them. And as she looked about she had to credit them to something altogether physical, irregularity of glands or corpuscles or gastric juices. Because what comfort would there be for her in this French business-house? Assuming she needed comfort. She had not come away for it, she had simply come away, and if she were to look back now it would be too soon for anything to be resolved. Time, a distance of time, was the essential factor. The most she could hope for was that when she went back she would have no more questions to ask.

But where was the promise—here? The air of permanence was Balto's business climate, it could have no significance for her. The rest was walls and windows, nice, serene old walls, and a group of people to whom she owed nothing and with whom she had nothing in common beyond this place and time. She was, she concluded, herself putting out the promise, hope, comfort, whatever it was, and getting it back like a full echo—the only known stimulus, she thought with amusement, being a teaspoonful of gin.

"You smile, madame" said old Cavour. "What amuses you?"

"Not amuses—pleases," she said tactfully. "I was admiring your offices."

Cavour opened his hands as if the place had blossomed out of them. "Ah, indeed, this is a beautiful building. It was occupied for many years by Henri Pecuchet. Here he made two fortunes, two great fortunes, and spent them." Cavour sighed. "I should be so happy to make one little one."

"You can count on that, surely?" said Antrobus, smiling.

Cavour's cheeks hollowed like a lantern. "In France, today? Today only the Government makes a fortune. The big flea is on the little fleas' backs."

"I should feel worried if I thought you couldn't handle that."

"But what has become of us? Pecuchet would not be possible today, if he were to make such money he would see it only on paper. No aeroplanes, no racehorses, no yachts, no safaris—"

"It is becoming true," said Bonnetante, "that to earn a hundred francs you must first spend a thousand."

"Who will work for paper?" cried Cavour. "Even I, an old man without pleasures, must work for something—a little money to keep body and soul together and to bury me when they come apart."

Madame Cavour remarked that Rose looked German.

It was an odd moment, they all turned and considered Rose. She was abstracted, cut out from their dubious kinship. In that moment she felt they had settled something on her.

"Actually my wife comes from Beckenham," said Antrobus.

"Beckenheim? It is a German name," said Madame Cavour. No one corrected her.

Cavour raised his glass to Rose. "I have remembered something to tell you, madame, of the history of this place. During the Occupation a man was hiding a long time, perhaps a year, in the wash-cupboard—the lavabo. At the top is the basin and taps, so: underneath is the pipe in a little cabinet. In this cabinet he hid. The building was full with rubbish, no one living here save this one. He was Polish, Dutch, Russian, perhaps a lunatic. Some say he was only frightened. In this cabinet he curled like a serpent—"

"Round the waste-pipe?" said Antrobus.

"Like a dog," said Bonnetante. "He was called Bijou like a dog."

"In this cabinet he slept all day. At night he went across the roofs, he found some bread, he was not ambitious. Who was, in those days?" Cavour's beard arched to a winning smile. "It is true I was never in Paris then. I was in Switzerland, with good friends. I had food, clothes, daylight. I had only to please myself. But I was not pleased, I could not be happy. My heart bled for my country, every mouthful choked me because there were people in France eating dirt.

179

Every kind word was a blow because in France women and children were punished with death. Every hour of freedom was a mockery because I was confined—here." He tapped his forehead. "I was Occupied."

"En effet," said Madame Cavour, "il était désolé."

"This one, this Bijou, he too had only to please himself and he was pleased. In his cupboard no one could come behind him, he was content. Imagine, it was his shell, he did not wish to stand upright. Ah, the happiness of being able to turn one's back! Then at last Paris was liberated, Paris was free and there was no longer need to hide. But he would not come out. Why should he? Out of his wash-basin he was homeless—naked, madame," said Cavour delicately, "if you will think of a hermit crab."

"What happened?" asked Antrobus.

"They had to smoke him out. Then it was his turn to choke. There was always this one," Cavour said to Rose, "who was sorry to be free."

Bonnetante sighed, first gathering the air into his huge skin and then letting it rustle out with a noise like a tree turning its leaves. "Crossing the Champ de Mars he died of exposure."

They all laughed. Except Rose. She supposed that the story had all along been funny and laughter was now in order, was due.

"I'm sorry," she said to Cavour, as one who cannot pay a small fee.

"You don't like stories?"

"I thought this one rather cruel."

"Cruel? To myself?"

"To Bijou it was rather kind," said Antrobus. "He had the best days of his life in that wash-cupboard, it was a return to the womb, the only place one can be completely happy."

Rose turned her back. "I have a mundane sense of humour."

Cavour flung his arms wide as if to embrace her. "Madame, you should never ask pardon for a kind heart."

When the party broke up to go to the restaurant for

180

dinner, Antrobus said she had been too sharp with the old man.

"I don't like him. He's insincere."

"Well?"

"All that talk about suffering for his country. He was still having the cake that he'd eaten in Switzerland."

"I've no business with his morals, and neither have you. Will you come off those hassocks!"

"Must I laugh when he crooks his finger?"

"My dear girl, it was only a story and palpably untrue."

"If it wasn't true, or funny, or interesting, why tell it?"

Bonnetante had arranged that after dinner they should go to a night club. Cavour and his wife dropped out of the party, taking their grandson with them. The old man pleaded weariness, but he looked as curling and lustrous as ever.

Rose was glad to see him go. For him Antrobus brought out his business side plus a tongue-in-the-cheekness to accommodate the snide in Cavour. She heard all through dinner the bogus bonhomie put up between them. It occasioned her certain qualms which she had had before and could expect to have again, but now she wondered whether they were symptomatic of more, between her husband and herself, than two ways about the same thing. Was a man who could enjoy Cavour's sickish humour and cap it, being expedient only? Was it an eye to another kind of business that he turned on Bonnetante's wife? Was it six of one and half a dozen of the rest with him? Could it be, with any man? He had to have a larger half and perhaps she should be prepared to find that this was it.

The club was somewhere in the Bois. Rose had never seen a more curious place. The motif appeared to be frustrated endeavour and misplaced strength. It reminded her of a nightmare in which one tried to run and was fixed to the spot. Untrimmed beams clambered up the walls, the black glass bar was supported on coiled iron like massive bed-springs and the light fittings were in sockets that would have carried railway sleepers.

"Why do they try so hard?" she murmured to Antrobus as they were taken to their table.

"I imagine it's not easy to be different and right too."

Bonnetante seated them at a floorside table with himself and his wife. "One is not annoyed here. The cabaret is often clever—and nice." He looked pressingly at Rose. "One cannot say this of everywhere in Paris. The décor is nice also. Distingué." He picked up a match-stand that appeared to be rivetted with coach-bolts. "Do you agree?"

"My wife is single-minded," said Antrobus, "but not necessarily a prude."

"Pardon?"

"And even that's a phase. It will pass. I've always found her ready to live and let me live with my inabilities intact. She's not really intolerant, you know."

"But I am not complaining!"

Antrobus smiled. "In England we say, 'Ah, but you should have seen my garden yesterday'."

If Rose had come in now and seen him suddenly without the time to grow on her it would have taken a moment to recognise him. He had his same tidy shape, adequate for all his reasonable purposes, not to be picked, for good reasons or bad, out of a thousand others, but there was a different man inside. He managed to change everything. The usually pale, rather flaccid face was brickish, packed for action. The dark chin had a business bloom and nothing was withheld in this man's eyes. He was ready to spill himself and her too if it would carry a moment.

She said, "Am I being difficult, Monsieur Bonnetante?"

He looked shocked. "Chère madame!" and Antrobus gave him a mock salute.

Rose felt uneasy. She understood that so far as she was concerned something was going awry. At this stage she had not expected to be much concerned. This stage was still essentially a business function and she was present as a social accessory. Her social duty apart, she had expected to be with Antrobus—that only, and certainly no less. When champagne was put before her she picked up the glass and drank, seriously and privately.

Antrobus was drinking whisky, not privately, leaning across to the next table to the rest of the party. They responded, smiling, toasting him, tossing up and defining words with their hands. Rose could not hear above the throbbing of the small orchestra. She told herself that the sense of what was being said would bear out the suspect look of it.

"I don't cry easily, either," she said to Bonnetante.

"Madame?"

"Humour's so personal." She was thinking that some people would find him comic, poor man, he had such a crumpet face—all those big pores and baked freckles and the buttery shine. "I don't like extremes, they're vulgar. I don't like vulgarity, do you?"

Poor man, he probably did, he probably wasn't equipped to like anything finer. She took another serious drink from the glass he had just refilled for her.

"You mustn't believe what my husband said about me. I may have disappointed him this evening and he would be chagrined, naturally. But it was unkind to call me single-minded when he meant that I had a one-track mind. It goes to show what a very, very little way he sees into it." She rolled the stem of the champagne glass between her finger and thumb. "It's terrifying—" here was what this evening had surely been designed to prove—"how little we want to know about each other."

Bonnetante had only just settled the bottle back in the ice-bucket but he took it out again without so much as the twitch of an eyebrow.

"I have made enquiries, madame, and am happy to be able to tell you—"

"Really, Monsieur Bonnetante," said Rose, "what about?" She heard herself laughing for the first time that evening. She thought, this really is funny. "I thought you were engaged on public, not private, relations."

"About the matter you are interested in." Bonnetante filled her glass and wiped the mouth of the bottle with the table napkin as tenderly as if it were a child's. "The famille Marigny."

Antrobus had asked Madame Bonnetante to dance. He called her 'Yvette'. Was that her name—like a French maid in a British farce?

"Maître Quentin Marigny is dead," said Bonnetante. "Of the family there remains his wife, Madame Marigny, living at Neuilly, and a daughter, a Madame Danièle. She has a boutique, a nice small business in rue Lapalisse near the Bourse. It is called 'Céline'."

"Chelle?" Chelle was the business woman. "Is she dark and small and quick like a monkey?"

"I have not seen these ladies, madame."

"There was another daughter—"

"There is no one else."

Antrobus danced badly, jigging against the rhythm and hustling his partner into other people's backs. He and Madame Bonnetante could be identified as a travelling eruption on the crowded floor.

"And Bonneval? They had a château at Bonneval, it would belong to Valentin now—"

"There is no one else now."

Chelle in rue Lapalisse, black little Chelle with no time for anyone or anything except money and the people she was getting it from, had the Bonneval noonday with her, she had those hours when the leaves took the weight of the sky and one blade of grass wagging was a signal in the stillness and the towers shone like tin and at table the family watered their wine. Chelle had the forest, she *was* the forest. Thirty years after I can't remember all those canyons, galleries and torrents of trees except as Chelle. It's not surprising that she should emerge as the spirit of the place. She imposed herself on it because she was strong enough and the only one who cared enough to do so.

I found I could visualise Chelle as a woman. She would have grown up smart, her hair that used to have sawdust in it would be tinted an unsuitable colour. She would pretend not to know me, perhaps she really wouldn't remember. It would make no difference. She was always so taken up with her own affairs she would in any case be unaware of any but the barest facts even about her own sister.

Solange I couldn't imagine as other than she had been. I certainly couldn't see her at my age—not that there was anything Peter Pannish to go on—I simply didn't see her getting to it. She would have died first. And it would be beyond Chelle or anyone to tell me how she died. All I could hope to hear now was what terminated her life and I could draw my own conclusions, which I would have had to do anyway. Alive and talking Solange would never have told me what I needed to know.

As Bonnetante had said, 'Céline' was a good business. I wouldn't have bought anything there without first fixing a reserve price in my mind and it would need to be steeper than I normally pay. Not that I'd be tempted, I don't know who would—rich women perhaps, for their trousseaux, actresses, what used to be called the demi-monde. The things were exquisite, made with artistry and of the finest materials. With a woman inside them they would be obscene, she would be better covered by a spider's web.

I tried to decide what to say to Chelle. She had never been easy to talk to, as a child she was already older than everyone else. She could brush me aside, she had been good at that and would be better still now. Although she could hardly refuse to answer my questions she might answer them so that I was left with new ones. I didn't want to go to Madame Marigny, her cloud of unknowing would surely have become a fog.

I walked past the shop and looked into a confectioner's window. Facing Chelle didn't worry me so much as facing what she stood for. I've always regarded Bonneval and the Bonneval summer as the making of me.

I decided that attack was my best method of preservation. I decided to tell Chelle right away that she would not recognise me and that I didn't require her to. I would tell her that it would be enough if she would cast her mind back to recall that there had been such a person as Rose Tedder and would accept me as that person and indulge my legitimate curiosity for five minutes.

I went into the shop and a man, tall and languid, drifted to me, smiling. He took one look at my feet and asked in English if he could be of service.

"I'd like to see Madame Danièle."

He was sorry, Madame Danièle was just then otherwise engaged. Was there something he could show me?

"I'll wait. It's a personal matter."

He had beautiful eyebrows which he used to identify his reactions. His smiling jaws, like his black coat and striped trousers, were de rigueur. The rest of his face did not move.

He bowed me to a gilt chair. I should take a seat—it might be one moment, it might be ten before Madame Danièle was available. Certainly he would acquaint her, but with what name?

"She doesn't know my name. I'm a friend of her sister's."

His eyebrows crept a shade higher. "A friend from America?"

"From England."

Why America? What was he thinking? Was it native caution or something specific that made him hesitate? Or was he registering details to pass on?

He went away smiling his dress smile and I looked at the shop. It was all dove-grey and gold, a small place, 'intimate' I suppose it would be called, lined with tinted mirrors. I could see my head and shoulders in them. My hat, which had looked smart when I put it on, was now entirely me, the emphasis misplaced on aspects which did not bear on the matter in hand. For instance, a tendency to what, in a younger woman would be fluffiness, in me was a smudging of outline. I've always wanted to be clear-cut. At my age it would even be preferable to be a little haggard. People have said that my name suits me, and what can be worse than a middle-aged rose?

My hat was wrong that day, so was my oatmeal-coloured suit—there was surely never such a colour for spreading. And my amber necklace, perfect with the suit, was perfect for any number of occasions excepting this one. I nearly went away, I felt at such a disadvantage. Then I comforted myself that I wasn't seeing a true image because the mirrors were tinted and I turned to the showcases.

In one of them a night-dress was trailed from the beak of a crystal bird. It gave me a curious feeling as if I, not the garment, was being offered for sale. It was scarcely a garment, it was designed to accentuate a woman's nakedness and I would cheerfully have paid for the satisfaction of stuffing it into the fire.

A woman appeared at the back of the shop. I saw at once that it was not Chelle. She was tall and moved deliberately—painfully, I dare say. She had the sort of figure which at her age can only be achieved by corsetting. Her hair was dyed the colour of peach dust and wound round her head like a turban. She carried one hand within the other, which most women do out of awkwardness. She did it out of self-possession. She was a complete stranger.

"Madame Danièle?'

When she nodded I said, "Née Mademoiselle Marigny?" and she did not bother to nod. I had to face the fact that Bonnetante's enquiries had gone wide. It was the last thing I had allowed for. I wanted to find out where the mistake was, but in my embarrassment it did not occur to me that this woman might understand English. I felt myself colouring up, swelling with colour as I used to when a girl. My French sounded pidgin and vulgar.

"Mais vous n'êtes pas, je suis sure, la fille du Quentin Marigny, le Maître Marigny de Bonneval?"

"La même."

I don't think I've seen anyone else off the stage or screen wearing such a zealous make-up. It was a dense mask, almost a fabric, with the skin pores showing through like the weave. Shadows were feathered in under the cheekbones and laid greenish and moist on her eyelids. Her mouth was boldly shaped, impossible to see how much of it was her own. Her lashes were stubbed with mascara, the shape of her eyes lengthened and changed with it, all I could see of them was a glimmer, a sign, no more, of occupancy.

It must have taken hours to put that face on, it was

grotesque and misleading as a clown's. How should I know that it misled when I'd never seen her before?

"Rose-red," she said, "comme d'habitude."

I couldn't believe it, I couldn't believe anyone could hide so completely. I kept trying to place something of hers, but only the way she looked at me was unmistakable.

"You have improved, Rose, but you still have too much blood in your neck."

I touched the beads at my throat, lifted them and felt myself as absurd as an immensely fat woman whom I once saw perspiring and slapping her chest with a rope of pearls. It convinced me that this was Solange.

"What ashames you?" She widened her eyes, the glimmer became a glint of laughter. "There was always something, so what is it now?"

"I'm sorry." It was ridiculous that I should have to stop myself straightening and twitching and trying to divert her attention from my face when God knew it was my own and I had nothing to be ashamed of. "I didn't expect to find you here, I expected to find Chelle—"

"The shop is named for her."

"I didn't expect to find a man here—"

"Lutèce, my partner."

"It was a shock seeing you—I mean," I said hopelessly, "when I'd thought—Solange, I'm so glad, so very glad."

I would rather it had been Chelle, anyone—not even a Marigny. Solange had never let me be, I had always to watch with her and suffer, by myself, my own normal legitimate actions turned antic. I did not like her, but it had taken thirty-five years to assemble discomfitures, mischiefs, reservations and inadequacies into that plain fact which wasn't going to help me now.

"Chelle is in America, Valentin is dead and my father also. There is still Maman and myself to be glad for."

"Did Valentin—was it in the war?"

"He did not need the war, he did it himself."

"You don't mean he committed suicide?"

"He died with food poison." She took one hand out of

the other and spread it with a touch of the old impatience. "If you wish to talk we can go to the office."

The man, Lutèce, was in the room behind the showcases. I fancied he had just moved from the door. If so, he had been listening. He and Solange did not speak, he passed us, smiling, and swayed away into the shop.

The room contained a desk, armchairs, and in an alcove a divan bed. Solange watched me look at it.

"You know what you must think, Rose?"

"I beg your pardon?"

"You were always so pure in the heart, since then you have been given to think." She turned her back to take a bottle and glasses from a cupboard. "Even if I tell you that sometimes I sleep here, sometimes I do not go home, you won't believe me. Once you had no doubts, now you have them and you give no one the benefit."

"I really don't know what you mean."

She poured a cognac and pushed it across the desk to me. She did not smile as she used to—I think the glaze would have cracked on her face—but it was still my drawback to be aware that she was getting the same sort of entertainment out of me.

"I can't believe you've changed sufficiently to care what other people think."

She drank her cognac and poured another. "Do you never exercise your own thoughts?"

"I didn't come here to quarrel—" But it was needless to say because she never quarrelled. "Or to argue the point."

"What point?"

"I came out of friendship."

She sat down in the chair opposite and with the toe of each foot prised off her shoes. They had heels like pencils.

"I wanted to know what happened to you all. Is that suspect?"

Of course it was. Everything I said and did was for re-examination to make holes where she could not find any. But suddenly, as of old, she had had enough. She turned her mask towards me.

"This is what happened. My father died, Valentin also.

My father was already old. Chelle married a life-saver and lives in Florida."

"A life-saver?"

"They have a house on the beach. Tin-Tin is dead many years, so is Uncle Dubosque. What else? Maman and I live at Neuilly."

"With your family?"

"I have no family."

She was pouring her third brandy. I hadn't touched my first.

"You married—you're Madame Danièle?"

"Je suis veuve."

Yes, she had had enough. She was ready to drop everything outside herself. If I had stood up and said goodbye I believe she would have let me go without another word. And she would drink the brandy I had left. It should be possible to detect at least some tremor in the movements of her hands.

"And you had no children? Neither did I, though I'm lucky—I still have my husband."

"I'm glad."

She hadn't lost the old trick of cutting the ground from under me by suddenly taking her tongue out of her cheek.

"He's here in Paris. I'd like you to meet him."

The mask had tilted as if it was heavy on her neck. I remembered her saying once that no one should tell her what to do, she would always do as she wished. Presumably this was it, a part if not the sum of what she really wanted—to paint her face and drink alone.

"Why not come with me to the hotel for tea?"

She drained her glass and let her wrist drop with it on to the desk. Her fingers, uncurling, rubbed around in the direction of the bottle. She did not look at them but I don't think their deviousness was for my benefit.

"Are you writing a book, Rose?"

"Heavens no. Why?"

"Then you want us all in parcels with the string tied and labels—'This one is dead, this one will be dead soon, this one would be better dead.' "

"Why must you question everything I do? Do you serve everyone the same or am I the only one who isn't an ordinary human being? Is it so improbable that I should have ordinary human feeling? Some interest in my friends? Just enough to care what happens to them?"

"Poor Rose." A spasm passed over the mask. She must have been smiling, really smiling, under it. "I'll tell you what happened."

"Don't if you feel it's none of my business."

"It's as much yours as anyone's now." She picked up the bottle. "If you will permit me?"

"Who am I to stop you?"

"You are my old friend, Rose Tedder. But you have another name. What is it?"

"Antrobus."

"That is a sea bird?"

"You're thinking of albatross."

"Rose Antrobus. It becomes you." She pushed her glass aside as if she meant to take no more. "I had three children, two daughters and a son."

"Had?"

"They are dead in the war. They and their father."

"Solange, how terrible!"

"Yes, what happens is terrible. My husband was rich, a very quiet, good man who expected himself in everyone. He was a Jew, he did not practise his religion but he had a nose—so—" She sketched it on the air—"and everyone could see that Danièle was a Jew."

She had not cared for him. She was always an island and the sea round her had grown cold.

"You have friends, Rose? Are there ladies who call on you and ask, 'What should we do today? What should we play at—tennis, golf, cards?' At school you had so many friends."

"You had yours outside school."

She went and lay down on the divan, clasping her hands under her head. "We lived in Toulon and in Paris. Danièle was buying and selling, what you call real estate. Some of it was nice property, nice villas, hotels, shops. Some was

191

not nice, that was not his fault. He did not build it nor make slums or bordels of it. He was a quiet, good man," she said again. It sounded more like an excuse than a commendation. "Details are not necessary. In any case they are mine—yes, the details are my business."

I would have liked them just the same. I wanted to know what sort of house she had lived in, what she had done with her days, how often her husband was home. Did she think about those things? If not, what did she think about? What other details?

"When the war came Danièle would not leave, not even when the Germans came to Paris. He did not believe those stories about the Jews, he said there were always such stories in wartime, he said he had nothing the Germans wanted, they could take anything of his without taking his life."

I couldn't decide what impression she meant to give me. He might have been a fool, a hero or an abysmal coward. But one thing I was sure about: from this distance of time she was mocking whatever he had been.

"He was right. They took everything, all that was left was his life, and this they destroyed because they did not want it. A Jew's life," she said softly. "They came and fetched us, even the children, even the little boy, a year old, in a big white car, an American car. Danièle put such hope into it, he thought no harm could come to us in an American car." Underneath the mask she was smiling, really smiling. "They said he was a member of the Resistance, they said he was using his hotels and villas for small-arms factories."

"Was he?"

"It was a game. First they pretended not to notice that he was a Jew, then they pretended that they had nothing against Jews. And Danièle believed it. I don't know for how long—perhaps only until he came to Dachau."

She looked relaxed and peaceful lying with her hands under her head. I remembered how she used to lie on her bed at Winterthur because anything that we might do was not enough for her.

"And the children? What happened to them?"

"What happens to the children of a Jew?"

192

She propped herself on her elbow. It was horribly inadequate, all of it. I couldn't take her word, I wasn't sure that those children had even existed, or the man, or any such quiet, stupid man. I was being all I could be—polite. It was her own fault: the way she lolled there with her cardboard face tilted on her hand and her skirt rucked above her knees did not bear her out, it didn't relate. It was the wrong picture for the sound-track.

"Now we all know. We have read that what happens to children happens to men and women also. What else? There is only the worst and that is not for wood and stone, it is for flesh and blood."

"But they didn't—They let *you* go?"

"For me it was worse to let me go, and of course they wanted that each of us should have the worst."

She swung her legs off the divan, with moistened finger smoothed her stockings over her ankles.

She herself had said that the worst was for flesh and blood. Even at Winterthur, even at Bonneval there had never been more than a pretence of being that.

"Oh God," I said.

"God, I think, is satisfied."

"Satisfied?" I was spilling my untouched brandy. I put the glass from me.

She said, "Why don't you drink?"

I'm not good at consoling people. Naturally they want to be concentrated on and I don't seem able to get beyond saying how *I* feel, how sorry *I* am. She gave me no scope for the stock phrases even if I could have found them.

"Perhaps you prefer something else? English women like to drink gin and tonic. Or the Four o'Clock?" She peered at a watch lying on the desk. "But it is only half-past three."

"The Devil might be satisfied," I said, "if he existed."

"Que tu es encore enfant!"

It was also fairly childish to blame God, but she was entitled if not justified in putting the blame where she wanted. It would be presumptuous of me, thank Heaven, to try to chat her out of it.

"I've been—lucky." I couldn't say 'normal', and anyway

it wasn't quite the word. There had always been an element of performance for me in talking to her—now there was restriction too. There was so much I shouldn't ask, or answer, for fear of hurting someone badly hurt already. Although that's a conventional fear, people want to talk about their pains. In Solange's case it was hypothetical too.

"Was there no chance? One hears such extraordinary things—children saved and finding their families after years—I'd never give up hope."

She said, as if it was I who had to be handled, "That is the first thing you must do. If for this you cannot do penance, how should you escape a moment of it?"

"Penance?"

But she had dropped me and that was something else I remembered, wondering, furiously, if she had the choice, what piece of the world she would pick up to entertain her. She was palming both hands down her tight thighs, straightening her dress. She went to a mirror and leaned close into it. She seemed to be checking on the condition of every inch of the mask. What she could do with her fingertips, rubbing, lifting, stirring, she did, and I could see that they were so customary as to be automatic, almost reflex actions. I believe she would have had to do them in the dark.

I had no intention of being dropped.

"What did you mean, you can't do penance?"

"It was the wrong word. My English is not good."

"Your English is excellent."

"Then let us say I wish to spare you details."

"A penance satisfies the sinner, not God. Why should you want that sort of satisfaction?"

She was touching, with her curious blind precision, the pink turban of hair. If she didn't tell me I should think what I could. If 'penance' was the wrong word—and it always would have been wrong for her—what was the right one?

"I shall give you a present, Rose." She went to a shelf and took down a flat cardboard box. "Because you are always the same it shall be something that is not like you."

I had no opportunity of seeing what it was just then. She

took it out of the box and bunched it in her fist. When she opened her fingers it was to show me how the natural verve of the material caused it to spring from her palm. Other people might have jingled or tapped or played with something as they talked. She kept bunching and releasing the scrap of silk. As a matter of fact it was ridiculous the way it leaped like a live thing in her hand and it made what she was telling me peculiarly shocking.

"We all had to stand while they questioned Danièle, even the children—especially the children. That was part of the game. I had the baby to hold, he was unwell and the weather was hot, the sun was hot enough for me to smell the wood of the chairs and tables as if it had just been cut. For two hours, perhaps three, we were standing, they only had to take a drink of water for the children to suffer. Danièle kept asking if the children could sit on the floor, just five minutes, and he was told if he would show he was not of the Resistance we could all go home to bed. Danièle thought he had only to speak the truth. They pretended to be not quite convinced. He tried to prove how little he knew and then he tried to prove that he knew nothing, that he was an idiot."

She was smiling openly, stretching her mouth, and I suppose she usually avoided that because it must have been uncomfortable, the mask wasn't big enough.

"I knew that none of this mattered, it was a game until they were tired of playing. But I could not wait for that, my children were tired already, we had to hold them up or they must have fallen. What I did was the only thing to be done. Then, now, and in a hundred years I shall never know better."

"What did you do? What could you do that was so terrible?"

"You must understand there was also the heat of the moment. Such heat," she said smiling, "of the weather and the heart. There was nothing I would not do then to spare my children. So I cried out that I was not a Jew and neither were they."

"It was the truth—"

"And Danièle—what do you think Danièle said to me?"

It struck me that I had hardly ever heard her laugh, and Heaven knows she must have had a pretty private sense of humour to be able to laugh just then.

"He said, 'We are not on trial for our race'."

"How could he be so blind?"

She shook out the piece of silk she had been bunching in her hand and I saw what it was.

"I denied my husband to save my children and I saved only myself."

I can honestly say I shall never wear such a thing, I shan't even try it on.

The ladies were not disposed to be constructive. Their moods combined to a tacit though ragged opposition. Victorine and Mrs Choules were gossipy, Sue Betts was being Middle West, Mavis Tyndall did not open her mouth and Miss Havelock was grim. Watching them settle, Rose was disposed to be analytical.

It was no sudden affinity between Victorine and Mrs Choules causing them to put their heads together. Victorine was putting up a front—aware that she needed one, afraid of being pinned down and someone getting a long enough look to see what Victorine Gregory was made of. Sue Betts was proclaiming her difference, locating herself somewhere wide and handsome away from them all. The Havelock woman was waiting to refuse to be coaxed, and Mavis Tyndall was saving herself up. Some women found it impossible to be objective, it would be bad luck if Rose had a majority of them on her committee.

"Isn't the Reverend coming?" asked Mrs Choules.

"He has a deacons' meeting."

Rose had already decided that Cade's withdrawal from the Committee should come up when the business of the meeting was done. She had his formal letter setting out his reasons and intended to read it to them.

"I seem to remember he had scruples, too," said Victorine.

"I hope we all have," said Miss Havelock.

"That's a point." Victorine looked brightly. "One woman's scruples are another woman's headache."

"Hartley says we could invest Hilda's money while we're figuring what to do with it," said Sue Betts. "He says why don't we make up a syndicate and try the market."

"With forty-eight pounds?"

It was remarkable how a woman as fat as Miss Havelock could smile so thinly.

"That would be the basic, the pork strip sort of. We'd each put in something of our own, like we used to put flour, lentils, apple-rings, whatever we could afford, to our neighbourhood suppers."

"As the lowest common contributor I'm in favour, provided we each qualify for an equal share of the pot," said Victorine.

"We'd have systematical gains, of course."

"Meaning if I only bring lentils I only get lentils?"

"Honey, it wouldn't be all the same as a cook-up, but it would be a lot of fun."

"The money or the goods, that's my maxim," said Mrs Choules. "Nice it would look, wouldn't it, gambling with church money?"

"It's not church money yet. Remember?"

"Hilda would have been tickled pink to know we were playing the market."

Miss Havelock's distaste disassociated her. "What grounds have you for thinking so, Mrs Betts?"

"The grounds that I was a good friend of hers."

"Then I trust I shall have no good friends to read my mind after my death."

"I should think you're safe enough there—"

"We could make the profits, when there were any, over to the fund and stand the loss of our own stakes." Victorine said, "No one would object to our doing a wrong thing for a right reason—"

"We've unfinished business to attend to," Rose broke in. "Shall we begin?"

Miss Havelock held up a large palm. "May I say that if

197

this business is not finished this afternoon I shall attend no further meetings on the subject. I am a busy woman, I can't afford time for idle bickering."

"I'm sorry if we've bickered," said Rose. "Though I don't think it should be called 'idle'. We're conscientiously trying to settle a question and I have every hope that we shall settle it now."

"Then," said Victorine, "Mrs Choules must be joining the humanitarians."

"I can't join anything, dear, just now. I'm fully taken up at the end of the financial year."

"Didn't you say it would be cheaper to build a new church than keep furbishing the old one?" Victorine looked disappointed. "We already know there'll be boilers to replace, you said, and hadn't I noticed how the ridge tiles are cocked and the vestry floor is tenting like a piecrust—I took it to mean you intended to switch your vote. You're not one to throw good money after bad, you said, and I thought well, we haven't thrown any money, good or bad, at Mrs Peachey yet."

Mrs Choules turned mauve. "I never said nothing of the sort—"

"No one need back down," said Sue Betts. "As chairman Rose has a casting vote."

"Ah well, we know where that will go."

"As chairman," said Rose, "I am required to regard the casting vote as held in trust for the general opinion and not for a section."

Victorine smiled. "Here have we been, Miss Havelock, Mrs Tyndall and me, waving our little flags at the great stone faces. Wouldn't you know we'd be outnumbered by a technicality? Someone should tell the Peacheys we tried."

"It won't be necessary."

Mavis Tyndall was wound up and ready, now that she had been touched, to run on. And on, Rose thought. She had more than something to say, she had something to unload.

"None of it's necessary now."

"Why?"

"Mrs Peachey's gone."

"Gone where?"

"No one knows. She's left the district."

This was what she had been saving up for, believing she had blame to lay, believing they would feel the weight of it, as she did. Now she would go on, brooding and fretting and chalking up a cross for herself and for them—and bitterly having to bear it alone.

"We might have stopped it if we'd lifted a finger. We can't be sure of that, can we? We can never sit back and say there was nothing we could have done. I don't mean just *her*—if she'd only got herself to harm I'd say good riddance. I might say good luck because she'd need it and I'd sooner—we all would—not have to see her about. But there are the children. Their home's broken—what there was of it was theirs, they belonged. Oh yes," cried Mavis Tyndall, "children can belong with orange boxes and cracked china."

Rose had no intention of resigning them to the longueurs of this sort of thing. She said crisply, "What exactly has happened, Mavis?"

Mavis Tyndall wore a hat with a half veil, and it was this veil, trembling delicately with strain, that chiefly vexed Rose. Mavis Tyndall was a small woman who would impose her high soul on them all if she weren't prevented.

"Exactly? Mrs Antrobus, I can't tell you exactly what happened, I wasn't there. I wasn't told, I had to get to know."

Rose could appreciate how that would rankle—finding out, when all was done and done with, and not even a sixth sense to warn her.

"Through the police, the police if you please, coming across my name and address in the flat—because I'd told her to turn to me with anything that troubled her. Did I know, they said, where she'd gone? She'd have told me, they said, she'd be bound to because I was her friend—*her* friend!—and I could see they thought I was shielding her. They wouldn't tell me what had happened to the children. I had to go and ask the neighbours—"

Rose stood up. She disliked coincidence. There was no

need for Fate to tap her on the arm nor for history to echo itself inside a week.

"Nothing so terrible, surely, could happen to the children?"

"I would have thought," said Mrs Tyndall, standing up too and levelling her chin at Rose's top dress button, "that losing their mother was terrible."

"She didn't take them with her?"

"That would be no part of the plan," said Victorine.

"What plan?" cried Mavis Tyndall. "What plan could she have that didn't include them?"

Victorine blew cigarette smoke down her nose. "The plan any woman has when she wants to kick over the traces. It doesn't stretch to having the kids along."

Rose was beginning to understand that Victorine's vulgar streak had not needed to be acquired. It would account for Sam Swanzy.

"Where are they now?" asked Sue Betts.

"They've been taken into care—a Council home. You know what that means!"

"That's hardly fair," said Rose. "I'm sure they'll be well looked after. There are some very worthy people on the Children's Board—the Reverend Cade is one."

"Boards!" cried Mavis Tyndall as if it were an expletive. "Committees!"

Mrs Choules patted her hand. "I know what you mean, dear, children need their mothers. But some mothers don't deserve the name."

"So if we'd given her the money," said Sue Betts, "she'd have blown it on this spree."

"With some man—or men."

"When I talked to Mrs Peachey—Oh yes, I've been to see her," said Rose, "I reminded her that she had the children to live for. It wouldn't have been necessary with any other woman, but I got the impression that Mrs Peachey intended to live for herself."

"We don't know, we're not sure we couldn't have prevented it—"

"Obviously we couldn't when she was so ready to go," said Miss Havelock.

Victorine said idly, "What did she do about the kids? Leave them to fend for themselves?"

"She telephoned the police station—on her way she must have been then—and said there were three young children left unattended. Why didn't she ring me—I told her to—Anything she needed, I said. Why didn't she?" Mavis Tyndall, looking from face to face, was searching for Mrs Peachey's reason. She couldn't accept that she, who had involved herself, should have counted for nothing. And Mrs Peachey had neither known nor cared that she had a hold.

"It was the little girl—" She was childish herself, the way she looked up, even at Rose—"she needed—" She couldn't bring herself to say what the child needed, not to them. "She *needed*," she said hopelessly and went back to her chair.

"Of course we're all sorry about the children," Rose said. "They at least are innocent. But it does transform the situation we're immediately concerned with."

"People should not need paying to shoulder their responsibilities," said Miss Havelock.

"I don't understand women who abandon their children. I can make allowances for a lot of things—we don't know the half, I always say—but there's no two ways about being a mother. We learn that from the brutes," said Mrs Choules.

"What sort of home was it, anyway? They're better off with the Board than with a psycho father and a maverick for a mother."

"Mrs Antrobus was right—"

"Mrs Antrobus is always right," said Victorine.

Miss Havelock drew on her gloves. "I shall wish you ladies a good afternoon."

"You're going? Before we've settled anything?"

"It has settled itself. The bequest now goes to the church. There remains only the formal closure of the meeting. I am sure," said Miss Havelock without humility, "that it can be managed without me."

"Hilda would have been pleased," said Sue Betts. "She

201

always said her kneecaps wouldn't let her concentrate on her prayers."

"I don't agree." Rose picked up her minute-book and wrote 'Proposal' and ringed it heavily. "I think the money should go to the children."

"What?"

"You're not serious?"

"Is this your idea of irony?" said Miss Havelock.

Rose lifted her chin at them, but spoke mildly. "I know I'm generally supposed to be heartless, but I'm as concerned for these children as any of you. As I said, they're blameless. Giving them this money seems to me the least we can do."

"You're right," said Victorine, "about it being the least."

"What good would it do them?"

"It could be put into a fund until they are old enough to use it."

Miss Havelock lifted her lip. "Sixteen pounds, one shilling and fivepence each."

Rose looked at her directly. "It's a nucleus. Charitably disposed people can always add to it. I am formally proposing that Mrs Loeb's bequest for this quarter be donated to open a fund for the three Peachey children. Will anyone second that?"

"I will," said Mrs Choules.

Victorine groaned. "The needle's in the groove."

"Frankly I don't see how anyone can object," said Rose. "It's a Christian act."

Sue Betts shrugged. "I'm no Bible-pusher, but I'll go along with you."

"Mavis? What do you think?"

"Does it matter?"

"It would if you were against it." Rose said gently, "You, of all people."

"I'm not against it."

She had her chin buried in the dreadful little squirrel collar of her coat. She didn't realise how alienating sulks could be.

"If you're not against it you must be for it."

"No one can be against the motion, Mrs Antrobus, as you are well aware." Miss Havelock was really going. She paused at the door. "But between now and the next meeting I think you must decide whether this is to be a committee or a conversazione."

"Oh dear," Rose said when she had gone, "I thought everyone would be glad to be informal."

"She goes to Share meetings to relax herself," said Sue Betts, "and it's the ones with the smallest holdings that have to have the t's all crossed and the i's all dotted."

"I don't think I've had it all my own way, have I?" Rose smiled wryly. "It wasn't the general idea. I picked everyone for their capacity to see two sides of a question."

"It's nice we could agree in the end," said Mrs Choules. "Everyone's happy."

Rose glanced down at the crown of Mavis Tyndall's hat. "We shouldn't expect that even if it's passed nem. com. Now I think we'll break for tea. Will you excuse me while I fetch the trolley—Mrs Gibb isn't here today."

Victorine followed her. "I'll help you cut the cake."

"There's only the tea to make. Everything else is ready."

She didn't want help, Victorine's least of all. Not that she was going to get any—when they reached the kitchen Victorine went straight to the trolley and helped herself to a sandwich. She ate it while Rose switched on the kettle.

"You didn't ask me how I'd vote. You'd got your majority, of course."

"I intended to ask you. I don't take anyone for granted." Rose was annoyed to hear herself add, "Whatever Miss Havelock thinks."

"Bother you, does it?"

"Bother—no. What interests me," Rose was rearranging the sandwiches, "is how this suggestion of collusion could come up. Collusion I neither need nor want. If I did it would be spiking my own guns to form a committee. After all, I might have allocated Hilda's money without let or hindrance from anyone."

"It wouldn't have been such fun for you though." Victorine took another sandwich. "I didn't have time for lunch."

"I'm asking you," said Rose, "because you know as well as anyone—how I got this reputation for power politics."

"You like it, don't you? It's quite flattering and someone has to be the *force majeure*—you or Havelock. I'd rather be coerced by you than pulped by her."

"For Heavens' sake," said Rose, "all I wanted was an honest opinion out of any of you."

"Why did you change your mind about the money?"

She was perched on a stool, an éclair in her hand and her mouth full of sandwich. This was cosy chat, women's gossip, or something to do while she ate.

"Let's say my mind is flexible enough to appreciate a more pressing claim."

"It's not though, is it? Not more pressing, I mean. The kids will have to wait ten years for the money and according to you the hassocks couldn't wait ten weeks."

"Are we still arguing about it?"

"Of course you didn't so much want the church to have the money as for the Peachey woman not to." Victorine prised the top off the éclair. "I understand that. But I wonder why."

"It's become obvious, I thought, to the most gullible of us—which you are not."

"Giving the Peachey children the money would certainly seem a way of paying off my conscience." She put the éclair back on the trolley and took a strawberry tart. "Only they're not really on it."

"How nice for you."

"Should they be? I didn't break up their home and if she couldn't cope it was the best thing the poor bitch could do."

"Of course you'd think so. The best for her—and for who else?"

Rose was ready, at a look, to tell her, but Victorine chose not to put a personal interpretation on it. She said, twitching her sticky fingers, "And for the kids. That's why I'm surprised they're on your conscience. Give them the money? But there's nothing to pay. You know that as well as I do."

Rose poured an arc of boiling water into the teapot.

"I don't know what you know, Vee, and I'm glad. It seems unwomanly to be so hard-headed. Will you bring in the trolley? And for Heaven's sake let me close the case. Please! That's all we have to do now."

Arena

☐ The History Man	Malcolm Bradbury	£2.95
☐ Rates of Exchange	Malcolm Bradbury	£3.50
☐ The Painted Cage	Meira Chand	£3.95
☐ Ten Years in an Open Necked Shirt	John Cooper Clarke	£3.95
☐ Boswell	Stanley Elkin	£4.50
☐ The Family of Max Desir	Robert Ferro	£2.95
☐ Kiss of the Spiderwoman	Manuel Puig	£2.95
☐ The Clock Winder	Anne Tyler	£2.95
☐ Roots	Alex Haley	£5.95
☐ Jeeves and the Feudal Spirit	P. G. Wodehouse	£2.50
☐ Cold Dog Soup	Stephen Dobyns	£3.50
☐ Season of Anomy	Wole Soyinka	£3.99
☐ The Milagro Beanfield War	John Nichols	£3.99
☐ Walter	David Cook	£2.50
☐ The Wayward Bus	John Steinbeck	£3.50

Prices and other details are liable to change

ARROW BOOKS, BOOKSERVICE BY POST, PO BOX 29, DOUGLAS, ISLE OF MAN, BRITISH ISLES

NAME...

ADDRESS..

....

....

Please enclose a cheque or postal order made out to Arrow Books Ltd. for the amount due and allow the following for postage and packing.

U.K. CUSTOMERS: Please allow 22p per book to a maximum of £3.00.

B.F.P.O. & EIRE: Please allow 22p per book to a maximum of £3.00

OVERSEAS CUSTOMERS: Please allow 22p per book.

Whilst every effort is made to keep prices low it is sometimes necessary to increase cover prices at short notice. Arrow Books reserve the right to show new retail prices on covers which may differ from those previously advertised in the text or elsewhere.